TALISMAN FOR A SURGEON

Sister Rosalind Mason feels upset and humiliated
after her rows with the suave, elegant and eminent
surgeon, Peregrine Bradford. But as a friend warns
her, hatred is akin to love . . .

Books you will enjoy
in our Doctor–Nurse series

TALISMAN FOR A SURGEON

BY

LISA COOPER

MILLS & BOON LIMITED
London · Sydney · Toronto

First published in Great Britain 1982
by Mills & Boon Limited, 15–16 Brook's Mews,
London W1A 1DR

© Lisa Cooper 1982

Australian copyright 1982
Philippine copyright 1982

ISBN 0 263 73968 6

03/0882

Set in 11 on 12 pt Linotron Times

Photoset by Rowland Phototypesetting Ltd
Bury St Edmunds, Suffolk
Made and printed in Great Britain by
Richard Clay (The Chaucer Press) Ltd
Bungay, Suffolk

CHAPTER ONE

'You should know quite a few people here.'

'I don't know. A lot can change in one and a half years.'

'At Beattie's? You have to be joking.' Sister Wendy Fletcher laughed and tugged at the edge of her cloak that would insist on blowing back in the strong wind outside the Princess Beatrice Hospital in South East London. 'As I remember it, you left just after I came from Guy's.'

Rosalind Mason frowned. 'I shall have to think hard. Isn't it strange how some places fade in memory and work fills a person's life completely.' She was trying to recall faces and places, but it was difficult. 'If I'd trained here I would remember more, but I was here for only six months for midwifery training, and a part of that was done in Surrey.'

'But you liked it sufficiently to apply for the theatre job when the new ENT block opened?'

'Yes, I liked it here and was very impressed by the general efficiency and the friendliness of the staff.' She smiled as she passed the porter's lodge. 'Is Claud still here? He was a mine of information and had an inexhaustible supply of stamps.'

'Very much with us, is our Claud. He'll have your life history out of you in five minutes if you aren't careful, but he has his uses.' Wendy Fletcher glanced at the shuttered window. 'He's probably hanging around in Cas. again. He'll be hopping mad to hear that you arrived and he didn't see you.'

The two young women walked slowly to the entrance of the Nurses' Home. 'Have they re-built the medical hostel yet? Or do we still have strange men lurking in the corridors?' asked Rosalind.

'Only the registrars and senior house officers who need to be resident. No students allowed after eleven . . . when all sin shall cease.' She chuckled. 'Anyone would think that nothing could happen before eleven. Not that there's much chance of that in a place as busy as this. I haven't had time to go out on a date for ages. Either I can't get the right off-duty or I'm so bushed that I just have a bath and then put my feet up.' She glanced at the slim honey-blonde with the wide green eyes and wondered who was involved with her, suddenly regretting the incipient slackness of her own figure. 'I shall have to take up tennis again. I'm really out of condition.'

'That would be nice. I played a lot in the last hospital and I'd like to keep it up. There are courts here, I seem to recall.'

'We'll make a date.' She heard the clock strike. 'Haven't you to see Matron? Usual office in the old block. See you in the Home. I've no idea which room you have, but I can check from the board. Nice to see you again.' Sister Fletcher disappeared into the main entrance through Casualty, on her way to the children's ward over which she was in charge on day duty. Rosalind gazed after her for a moment, feeling like a new girl at a very large and intimidating boarding school. She shrugged and brushed her hand over the long sleek tress of hair that swung over her face and wondered if her duty hair style would have been more suitable for an interview with the most senior nursing officer in this famous hospital.

It was too late now, and why should she worry? She had been accepted for the post of theatre sister and should be considered sufficiently senior to decide how she looked in her off-duty.

Matron was ready to see her and the welcoming interview was pleasantly relaxed. It was obvious that her new status as a sister carried with it added trust as well as the additional responsibility.

'You have been here once for a short while. Do you remember any of the staff?' asked Matron. The wide polished desk gleamed softly and Rosalind thought how much more impressive it was than any of the sharply-cut modern office furniture in the new blocks. This was a part of the original hospital, built in Queen Victoria's reign, when marvellous materials were used and no expense spared to give an air of rich solid comfort and reliability. The deep-piled fitted carpet was warmly red and the curtains at the tall windows echoed the theme of rose, crimson and gold. Rosalind sat comfortably in her swivel chair and warmed to the woman across the desk, the room, the hospital and the fact that she was now a part of the great centre of healing that had served this part of London for so many years.

'I met Sister Fletcher on my way in, Matron. She recognised me because she had to come to the

midwifery unit when I was there, to fetch a child
who had to have an operation.'

'Now, who is there of your age group?' Matron
chewed the end of her pen. 'It's so important to
have a full and lively off-duty.' She looked shrewd-
ly at the pretty face, the lovely long hair and the
bright, widely-spaced green eyes and thought she
might be preaching to the converted. 'I expect you
have many friends, Sister, but as you know, hospital can be a lonely place until you sort out your
off-duty and can contact friends from outside.'

'I shall be fine. I'm used to hard work and get a
great deal of job satisfaction, Matron. I love music
and reading, so I can fill in the odd times when I'm
alone.' She smiled.

Matron glanced down at the folder on the desk
and saw that Sister Rosalind Mason had trained for
State Registration in a medium-sized hospital in a
country town. There had been no medical students,
as it wasn't a teaching hospital like the Princess
Beatrice, but her last post had been in a large
hospital when she worked as a senior theatre staff
nurse. 'Do you think you can cope with masses of
students all clamouring to watch cases? They can be
rather . . . overwhelming.' The flicker of a wicked
smile softened her words. 'As for our surgeons, you
may find them rather trying at first. They do a
magnificent and often daunting task, but they don't
suffer fools gladly.'

'So I hear,' said Rosalind Mason. Her full, soft
lips set into as firm a line as could be managed. 'I
think I can handle most situations, Matron.'

I hope you're right, Sister, I do hope so, thought

the woman who had watched pretty girls come and go, fall in love and be hurt . . . or find happiness and fulfilment in the work of the hospital or in a secure and satisfying marriage with one of the medical staff.

'Have you any special arrangements such as holidays, meetings with friends, that you would like us to honour before you get caught up in off-duty rotas?'

Rosalind looked at the interested, experienced eyes that regarded her so closely. She's really asking if I have a boy friend, she thought. 'I have no firm plans, Matron. My family are far away and I have no . . . attachments.'

'Frankly, you surprise me. If I may say so, you must find that you are attractive to men. I ask, not because I want to probe into your private life, but when a sister is appointed here with such good references, we like to feel that she will be with us at Beattie's for a long time.' She sighed. 'So many begin in a department with enthusiasm and skill and then they suddenly fall in love, marry and leave us.'

'That isn't likely to happen to me. I want nothing more than a satisfying career with no . . . hang-ups.' The bright green eyes looked into the deeply-set, friendly eyes and found understanding. 'I don't mind talking about it now, Matron, but I committed one of the deadly sins. I fell in love with a patient just after I began my training.' She bit her lip. 'Nobody told me of the dangers, and pity led to a very deep and traumatic love.' She saw the slight nod of encouragement and the smile that said that she understood and didn't condemn. 'I wanted to leave without finishing my training.' Rosalind swept the shimmering hair back again. 'I was so certain that I wanted nothing more of life than to give my time and strength to helping him. It was hopeless. He had a bad Addisonian crisis the day he should have left the hospital for the convalescent home and died before anything could be done.' Tears filled the green eyes. 'It was then that I knew I'd made a mistake. Other cases came in quickly and I had to work long after I should have gone off duty. When I rang his family, they treated me as . . . just a nurse who cared enough to want to enquire about the family wellbeing.'

'They were right.'

'Yes, they were right. I worked and in time, forgot, but I have never made the mistake since of becoming too involved with any man, patient or otherwise.'

'You will find someone, some day, Sister. Don't block the way to your true feelings, but keep the lesson learned that no involvement with a patient is a real human relationship. The drama of a sick ward colours everything, and we have all made that mistake at some time in our careers. There are other men, however, men with normal reactions to a pretty and intelligent woman, who have their health and strength and who may prove worthy of your devotion—not that you will see many here on duty except for your surgeons and their firms.'

'Who are the people working in ENT, Matron?'

'We have some of the best in London . . . in the world. The men who retired a few years ago were wonderful, pioneering surgeons, who laid the way for the young men with even more progressive ideas to take over and develop their work.'

'It sounds exciting.'

'It is. There is an atmosphere of excitement about your theatre. As you know, years ago a team of surgeons began operating with the aid of microscopes to do delicate operations on the ear. Mr Bradford has carried this work further and is fast becoming the foremost surgeon in this area. Of course, it isn't all micro-surgery. We still have the usual lists of ENT and childrens' T's and A's.'

'It sounds good. When do I have my first list?'

'Tomorrow. I suggest that you go up to the theatre today to get your bearings. There is nothing happening and your staff nurse will go through the cupboards with you. Do that now and this afternoon and go off for the evening to sort out your room.' She smiled again to show that the interview was over and Rosalind rose to her feet.

'I'll change into uniform and go now, and thank you, Matron.'

'One thing,' Matron frowned. 'There is a little friction between some doctors and theatre staff. Some doctors who act as anaesthetists for private cases outside the hospital have been taking hospital drugs and equipment to use elsewhere. It is forbidden and to be discouraged at all costs.'

'What happens if it is a senior man? I can't forbid one of the consultants, can I?'

'Oh, yes you can! They know the rules and if anyone is guilty—anyone at all—it must be reported to me or to the administrative nursing officer on duty. You must point out to the person concerned that you are doing this.' Matron laughed. 'Don't look so scared. Most of them try it once and find that the staff are wise to them and never do it again, but there have been cases where it has been a little difficult. I have no doubt that the firms using your theatre are above such things, but keep an eye open, as hospital equipment is costly and easily mislaid or broken in the wrong hands.'

Rosalind slowly walked back across the driveway to the Nurses' Home. In the car park near Casualty was the usual assortment of cars belonging to staff and visitors, including some battered old jalopies belonging to senior students and house doctors. She smiled. It was almost the same picture as the one she had seen the last time she came to Beattie's for her interview. She glanced further back to the park outside the private patients' wing. Even that was the same, with one impressive dark limousine parked by the main entrance. There was a steady stream of such cars that brought wealthy patients, visitors and consultants to the private block. Another big car came to a silent stop behind the first and she saw a tall dark man emerge from behind the steering wheel. He wore an immaculate suit of dark grey and the pale sunshine made free with the silk of his tie. Rosalind had time to note the athletic build and the controlled strength of his arms as he reached back for his black bag.

Unintentionally, her steps had taken her towards the car park, and she found herself looking over the narrow, low wall that separated the two car parks. The man straightened and glanced at the gold watch on his wrist. He looked up at the clouds scudding across the sky and reached back into the car for a tightly-rolled umbrella with a silver-tipped handle. Rosalind smiled. It would be a pity if he was sullied by a single drop of rain . . . such elegance and poise needed a silk umbrella! Her amusement was mixed with reluctant admiration. Soft wings of hair blew back in the breeze to reveal a touch of grey on the temples, the dark eyebrows lowered over piercing blue eyes and the cleft in the well-formed chin gave warning of firmness, power . . . ruthlessness.

He seemed to sense that he was being watched and the dark head came round to face her. For one moment, their eyes met and Rosalind put a hand on the wall to steady herself. It was as if a physical blow struck at her legs, or why would they feel weak? As if a message came across on the breeze, sharp and clear . . . a warning and a promise that they would meet again in some other sphere.

He stood for a moment, with a complete stillness that spoke of latent power and speed. He saw her smile and she blushed, knowing he saw it, and he wondered why a young woman with wind-blown hair should smile at a perfect stranger.

But I wasn't smiling at him, I was smiling because of him, she tried to tell herself, embarrassed to be discovered. She bent her head and the cascade of honey-blonde hair fell over her face, hiding her blush. She turned and walked to the Nurses' Home, without looking back. The stranger stared after her, watching the tight-fitting heather tweed jacket and misty purple skirt recede, the sweet line of youthful hips undulating gently above perfect sheer tights and well-polished high-heeled shoes. He slammed the car door and strode into the private patients' wing.

The new sister changed into the smart dark-green uniform that had been a jealously guarded privilege of Beattie's sisters from the time when Florence Nightingale had suggested the design of suitable uniforms for young ladies to wear while nursing the sick. The starched cap was easy to wear, although it took a little while for Rosalind to pin the ready-tied bow-ends to the top of her head before pinning the cap into place. She tugged gently at the lace bow under her chin and was pleased with the result. Uniform changed her appearance almost completely from the pretty, well dressed girl who wore ridiculously high heels and light colours and whose hair flowed freely over her shoulders or was caught up in a tie to cascade over her back like a pony tail. She looked in the mirror at the new face, devoid of any makeup but a touch of lipstick, the shining hair pulled back and up into a tight plait which lay neatly under the line of her cap, free of the short white collar on her uniform dress. The shining belt buckle, a present from her aunt, her sole remaining near relative, gave her courage as being something given with love. She hesitated and then searched in her trinket box for a long thin silver chain on which swung a disc. It was plain silver on the back and on its front bore the sign of the Yin and Yang, the sign of life, of male and female, with the Yin in silver and the Yang in ebony.

I wonder why I thought of it, she thought as she dropped the disc under her dress where it could be worn but not seen. My good luck charm, that I wore through school exams, hospital interviews and now on my first day here.

The main block echoed with hard shoes as the main body of visitors left. From the ENT theatre, it was just a sound in the distance, but the staff nurse looked at the clock.

'Do you mind if I go to lunch now, Sister?'

'Of course . . . you're off this afternoon, aren't you? It doesn't matter when I go, as officially I'm not on duty until tomorrow, but if you'd rather go to second lunch, I'll stay here when you go and give the keys to Nurse Bridges when she comes on this afternoon.'

Staff Nurse Stephen smiled. 'That's nice of you, Sister. That half hour makes all the difference to a trip up to the West End. Sure you don't mind going to first?'

'I shall be glad of a break. I can't take in any more cupboards for a while. I shall enjoy pottering about on my own this afternoon now that you have shown me the main supplies, Nurse.' She didn't add that this was another hurdle to cross. The thought of going into a dining room, with so many strange faces staring at the new theatre sister made her stomach churn. But it had to be faced and it might as well be now. She walked quickly to the lift and waited for the lights above it to change. It was on the ground floor and as usual, someone had left the gates open. She pressed the button and the lights changed. It stopped at the floor below her and showed no signs of coming up to her. She pressed the button again, but the person in the lift had made sure that there was a finger on the button before the doors closed and once more the lift went down . . . this time to the basement.

Sister Rosalind Mason sighed. More stairs! She ran lightly down the wide stairs at the side of the lift shaft and paused at each floor, wondering if the lift would be available. It was no use waiting, she decided, and ran down, having to pass the lift gates at every floor. As she ran, the lift rose and went up to the floor she had just left. Mildly annoyed, she watched it pass and saw who was standing there, seeming to fill the narrow space with his presence.

She kept going, certain that he hadn't seen her as she went by the wrought-iron cage. He was staring ahead, deep in thought and saw only the uniform of a sister of the Princess Beatrice Hospital hurrying by.

Oddly shaken, Rosalind walked across to the dining room and Sister Fletcher caught up with her. 'Hello! What's the rush? You going to first lunch? Good, glad I found you. It's mis. to go in alone the first time.' Cheerfully, she chatted as they collected food from the servery, and Rosalind tried to forget the impact of one very distinguished man with noble bearing and dark blue eyes.

'Thank you. I was dreading coming in alone.'

'Come over here.' Sister Wendy Fletcher waved to two sisters at a side table and walked towards them. Soon, they absorbed Rosalind into the small circle and she could eat and listen and smile as they exchanged hospital gossip and personal news. 'I thought Anna might be here today. She often has lunch here on the days when her husband has a morning list and picks her up after it.'

'I thought that it was taboo for staff to stay on as married couples,' said Rosalind.

'It's all right if they work in different departments. Anna was in gynae. when she met her husband, but as he was senior registrar in that theatre she switched to orthopaedics when they married.'

Rosalind frowned. 'Am I right in thinking there was a rather terrible man in charge of gynae.? I came across him when I was doing midder here. He didn't seem young enough to marry a sister here. I thought he was married, as a matter of fact.'

They laughed. 'You're thinking of Mr Slade Forsythe's *boss*. He was here when Anna and Slade married, but resigned shortly afterwards to do private work and to be an examiner for second MB and FRCS Vivas. They still consult him when anything tricky needs his experience and skill in diagnosis, and his bark is worse than his bite.'

'Does he operate here at all?'

'He has a small private hospital with other surgeons but comes here for the odd one. Slade became the new consultant and is now in charge of the unit.'

'How nice to have someone like Mr Forsythe to work with,' said Rosalind, wistfully. 'Matron didn't tell me who the chief is on ENT, but I suppose it's still Mr Collins.'

Wendy Fletcher stared and then laughed. 'You poor soul, you really didn't know?'

'Know what?'

'Mr Collins left ages ago. There was quite a change-round about the time you were here last. You have someone quite different. Let's hope you feel strong.'

'You *are* teasing me?'

Wendy stopped laughing. 'Of course we are.' But she refused to meet the troubled gaze of the green eyes. 'He's very good, the best we have, I'd say, and very good-looking. Slade Forsythe made enough ripples when he was free, but Mr Bradford . . . well, you just wait until you see him.'

'So he's efficient and not repulsive,' said Rosalind, lightly.

'He's dedicated to his work, a wonderful surgeon and very well liked by all the staff who work for him,' Wendy said.

'So what's wrong with him?'

'He has absolutely no time for women . . . unless they wear uniform and do *exactly* as he tells them.'

'Come off it, Wendy, he's not like that,' said one of the others. 'He's fair and just and gets a little impatient with junior nurses who look at him adoringly and drop everything as soon as he approaches.'

'Well, for goodness' sake, tell me the truth. What am I in for? Is he an ogre who eats new sisters for breakfast?'

Wendy chuckled. 'That's the point. You'll never get near enough to him to have breakfast. He lives for his work, has a good social life, but keeps all women just that tiny mile away from him.'

'He's not . . . ?'

The three women laughed aloud and several of the nurses at other tables stared. 'Don't even think it,' gasped Wendy. 'Imagine anyone hinting that Peregrine Bradford could be anything but very . . . very, overwhelmingly male. He even has me panting after him at times, and I'm fully booked.'

Rosalind finished lunch, went to the home, briefly, to tidy her already perfectly neat hair and cap, and strolled back to the theatre. The lift was now available and she went in and pressed the button for the right floor. It silently rested level with the floor and Rosalind contrasted it with some of the old lifts she had struggled over with wheel chairs and trolleys that had a deep step to negotiate when the lift stopped at just the wrong level. These doors slid quietly, too, making the general sense of peace complete.

The door to the instrument room was slightly open and she went in, expecting to see the staff nurse. One of the wide glass cases built to house the many surgical instruments and pieces of complicated equipment necessary for a busy and forward-looking theatre was half empty and instruments lay on a trolley in front of the case. Sister Rosalind Mason frowned. She called 'Nurse Stephen?' and went into the main theatre. Staff Nurse Stephen was talking to the nurse who was to relieve her off duty. She smiled.

'Is there a case today?' asked Rosalind.

'No, Sister. I was just telling Nurse about the instruments needed for a fenestration.'

'So I see. It's a beautiful set. By the way, where is the operating microscope kept?'

'There are two. One lives out there with that set and the one in general use is in this cupboard.' She glanced at the clock and asked if she could go.

'Of course,' said Rosalind, quickly. 'Have a good afternoon. I'll be here for a while and I'll wait until you come back on duty, in case I have any problems.'

She wandered back to the array of delicate instruments lying on the shining glass trolley. She picked up a small case in which lay, on a bed of velvet, some of the smallest and finest probes she had seen, the product of first-class workmanship and surely a joy to use. Tiny scalpels with angled handles lay in another case, dental instruments adapted for use in other small apertures in the inner ear, swab holders of Liliputian size, and every item necessary for the safe and skilful operation that so few people could perform. The junior staff nurse followed her, carrying a square black case such as doctors or surgeons used for the transportation of instruments and drugs. She began to pack the instruments into the case, checking everything against a list to see that it was all there.

Rosalind watched, puzzled. It was her first day as sister. Not even that—she wasn't officially on duty until the next morning. She had no right as yet to query anything she saw in the theatre unit. All she should do was to look and learn and take note.

The nurse worked on with pursed lips as if under stress. At last, she sighed. 'I think that's all. He took the microscope earlier.' She looked at the new sister as if hoping that she would check and so relieve her of the responsibility of putting a full set of instruments into the bag.

'Who took a microscope? I thought it was forbidden to remove anything from the theatre?' Anger and alarm mixed to cause her to raise her voice.

'It's Mr Bradford, Sister. He always takes the instruments and the microscope when he does a private case in a nursing home or if he is needed for an NHS case in a hospital where they haven't our facilities.'

'That's ridiculous. These cases are never so acute that they can't be transferred to a specialist unit. He has no need to take them to another hospital.'

'But what about the nursing homes? He always takes them. I was told to put them out and he collected the bulky stuff earlier.' The girl was almost in tears as she watched the new sister open the case again and carefully take out the velvet-lined boxes. 'He'll be furious,' she said. 'Please Sister . . . you shouldn't . . .' Her voice tailed away.

'If I am to be in charge of this theatre, I have to look after its interests. Matron told me today that no equipment must leave the departments, even if it is for a consultant, unless they have official permission from the hospital board.' She continued to unpack.

'Sister . . .' It was a cry of despair. 'Please listen. I know he'll hit the roof if he doesn't have that bag packed exactly as he wants it.'

'It's all right, Nurse. I take full responsibility.'

Who was this man who could reduce a nurse to jelly even in his absence? Who had the nerve to be angry if he was prevented from removing hospital property when he had no right to do so?

'Oh . . . please tell her.' Rosalind heard the nurse talking and the deeper voice of a man in reply.

'Is that Mr Bradford?' she called, coldly.

A figure lounged in the doorway. She breathed a sigh of relief. The sisters in the dining room had been teasing her. This man was of medium height, with sandy hair thinning on top and a rather vague, humorous expression. He was nothing like the description given of him. She could handle this one easily.

'What are you doing?' he asked, mildly.

'Putting these back where they belong. They have to stay here. I'm sorry, Mr Bradford, but I was instructed by Matron to make sure that nothing was taken away and used without permission.' She paused. He had said nothing. Was it a sign that he knew he was in the wrong and could make no excuse? 'Where were you taking them? Couldn't you do the operation here?' she said in a milder tone.

'Don't look at me.' He laughed and winked slowly. 'Let me introduce myself. I'm Tony Murray, senior registrar for this firm. I just brought up the list for the morning.' He laughed. 'I shall be doing the list . . . nothing much more than a SMR and a few tonsils.' He eyed the pile of boxes. 'Just a word of advice. Get those back in his case. He's on his way. No messing.' He shook his head and walked to the door, still grinning. 'I'd love to stay, but I can't stand the sight of blood.'

A cold hand seemed to clutch at her heart as the first glimmer of indecision struck her. What if he had received permission? 'Nurse? Has Mr Bradford been given special permission to take these things?'

The girl looked alarmed. 'He doesn't need permission,' she said. 'He *is* the department.'

Footsteps came crisply through the main theatre. Steps of someone sure of himself and in a big hurry. The nurse slipped away and the new theatre sister was left alone with the case half empty. As he came into the room, Mr Bradford switched on the extra light, flooding the room with cold brightness. 'I'll take my bag now, if you are ready, Nurse.' The voice was cool but pleasant, but edged with authority. It was the voice of a man used to giving orders and expecting them to be obeyed. He stopped as he saw the slim back of a figure in dark green. 'You must be the new sister. I didn't expect you until tomorrow.'

'I am officially on duty in the morning, but I came to get used to everything . . .' The cold light made his eyes grey-blue in the stern face. He seemed to be making an effort to be patient.

'Where is that nurse? I thought she would have finished ages ago. I told her to have it all ready by one-thirty and now it's two o'clock. I have a case to do in an hour and these have to be sterilised.' He strode past her as if brushing a fly from a curtain, calling for the nurse who was hiding in the sterilising room.

'Mr Bradford . . .' Rosalind's mouth was dry as she forced the words to come. It was the man in the grey suit . . . the man who had dominated her with a glance across a car park and who now showed no sign of linking the woman with long fair hair with the soberly-uniformed theatre sister with whom he had little patience. 'Mr Bradford.' He turned. 'I unpacked the case,' she said, clearly. 'I was told that no equipment could leave the department without special permission.' Why didn't the ground open and take her in? Why didn't a thunderbolt come and strike the figure who looked at her as if he could take her and crush her between his hands?

'You realise that I shall be delayed . . . a patient will have his anaesthetic delayed and a theatre booked for a certain time will be disrupted?' The voice cut across the silence with swift small slices of pain and the eyes glowed with fury. 'I have no idea who told you such ridiculous things . . . Sister.' The last word was almost an insult, dismissing her as someone unworthy of the name. 'I happen to own this equipment and the special microscope that goes with it. I bought them because the hospital instruments were not fine enough for certain procedures and I take them whenever I want them . . . is that clear?'

She lowered her eyelids so that he wouldn't see the hurt in her eyes. 'I thought . . .' she began.

'If we are to work together—and it seems as if we must—please don't think, just do as I tell you.'

She flushed with anger, her natural spirit surfacing.

'Just do . . . as you . . . are . . . told.' He was placing the cases back in the black carrier again. He snapped down the lid. He glanced at her with expressionless eyes. 'Now the drums,' he said. The nurse came softly behind Sister Rosalind Mason and held two drums of sterile swabs and towels ready to follow him to the lift.

Rosalind broke the icy silence. 'At least the drums are hospital equipment,' she said, triumphantly. 'You don't own everything here, I suppose?'

His face darkened. 'I need them for the case.'

She regained confidence. 'And you are taking hospital equipment.'

He hesitated, a hint of reluctant admiration in his eyes which he swiftly hid. 'I use *my* precious instruments in this hospital for the help of general, non-paying patients . . . so I take sterile swabs.' He gave a short laugh. 'Ask Matron. Even she considers it a fair exchange.'

He picked up the case and nodded curtly to the nurse to follow him. He regarded Rosalind as if seeing her for the first time. 'Haven't we met somewhere?'

'No,' she said.

'I think we have . . . I shall remember some day.' He smiled with all the warmth of a panther about to kill a victim with one soft strong paw. 'I have a feeling that I didn't like you very much on that occasion . . . whenever it was.'

'And I am sure that I would have remembered anyone as . . . charming as you,' said Rosalind, her face pale and small under the starched cap. She could feel the pull of her medallion as it caught on the strap of her bra. He turned away to the lift and she heard the faint whine of machinery. She shrugged to free the medallion. You didn't bring me luck this time, she thought, and sank into a chair in the office, limp and sad; not because she had inadvertently made a mistake, but because a pair of steely eyes had bored through her like destroying laser beams, with no warmth, no sign of wanting to know her.

CHAPTER TWO

SISTER Rosalind Mason glanced at the double glass doors over the instrument cupboard and saw that the full set of delicate instruments was still missing. Her heart thumped wildly with sudden panic. Perhaps Mr Bradford would bring them back while the theatre was busy and he would humiliate her again, in front of her new staff. She braced herself, forcing her mind to think of nothing but the list of operations that she held in her hand.

'Not too bad for your first day, Sister.' Tony Murray grinned at her as he tied a mask over his face and pulled the green theatre cap more firmly over his brow. 'I'm glad that the first one signed the consent form. He's been needing this operation for months but refused to come in. At last, the weather beat him. All those nasty east winds this winter made his sinuses fill up and he can hardly breathe with that deflected septum.'

'One SMR, one nasal polyps and five tonsils and adenoids. How many dissections?' She was calm again, relieved to have this pleasant, slow-speaking man to deal with and already beginning to enjoy the first day in her new theatre.

'Two dissections of tonsils. The girl is just too old for a snatch and the other is a man of twenty-four.' He grinned. 'He'll have a rather sore throat tomorrow, but no worse than the perpetual sore throat he seems to have had for the past year or so. I tried to tell him that this might be the last of his discomforts and I hope I'm right.' He glanced at the list that the junior nurse had pinned to the board. 'One of the tonsil cases is a red-head. Have you some coagulant ready?' He glanced round the shining theatre at the neatly-covered trolleys and the row of surgical dishes on a well-lit glass shelf at one side of the room near the stool where the anaesthetist would sit during operations. From that stool, whoever was administering anaesthetics could supervise the drawing up of drugs and the emergency use of haemostatic drugs. The light shining on the shelf was sufficient to let staff check such drugs in safety, while avoiding lighting the whole theatre during one of the cases where a blacked-out theatre was essential.

Rosalind knew from her own experience just how important it was to have a clear view of equipment at all times and smiled ruefully when she recalled one theatre in her own training school where the unfortunate nurse or sister who scrubbed-up to assist at ENT sessions had to grope around in the dark and just hope that she was handing the right equipment. A torch held by a junior nurse was never satisfactory and it was trying for the nursing staff and the surgeon who often had the torch shone on him by mistake by a junior suffering from a fit of nerves!

Here, the theatre seemed to have everything. Bright central lights which gave a brilliant, shadowless light over the patient on the table, side lights for use when semi-darkness was needed and the small spotlights for use when delicate operations on the ear and nose were in progress and the surgeon needed to see a restricted area lit only by his own headlight or reflector. The operating tables were fitted with expensively silent mechanisms to change the tilt or position of the table easily and safely. Slots to hold the base of the microscope were slim and close so that they didn't impede the surgeon in his work, allowing him to stand close to the table without lumps of steel digging into his stomach while he tried to concentrate on the job in hand.

There were no windows in the theatre or auxiliary rooms, but at the back of the small office was a window leading to a balcony where plastic sheeting could be left to dry or the theatre mops could drain after a list. It also had a bench fixed to the wall and on fine days the nurses could drink coffee there if there was no time for a break in the canteen. But there was no time to think of such luxury today. 'I've put out ampoules of Ethamsylate and Menaphthone Vitamin K and checked that we have a supply of Factor VIII,' she said.

'Well done. We haven't had a case of haemophilia here, but it's as well to be ready.'

'There was only one ampoule of 500 units. Do you think we should risk ordering more? Does it deteriorate very fast?'

'It's expensive at five pounds fifty for that dosage, but I think we should have more as that isn't the maximum dose and when we do need it, we'll need it in a hurry.'

'I've plenty of Adrenalin Hydrochloride and a few proprietory drugs that seem to be in a special box with a list of names.'

'We use them on selected patients and note the results. They've all been accepted by the Health Authorities as safe to use, but each patient is different and may react off-centre and show where the drug may mis-fire.'

'First case coming up,' said Rosalind, and went to her office to leave her cuffs and cap. She dressed in the usual theatre gown of green cotton and tied her hair up under the all-concealing matching cap. She was amused to see that the men's caps were the usual design of ill-fitting limp shapelessness. The female caps were smaller and gathered slightly to allow room for the often thick hair of female nurses or doctors. Yet another me! she thought. First the girl with long hair and not a bad figure, who can wear what she likes when she likes off duty, then the sister in that rather good uniform, the well-tailored dress and neat collar, the pretty cap with the hand-made lace bow under the chin and now . . . a being with no visible hair, no visible figure and no visible feet! The rubber boots were ones she had brought with her, knowing from experience how tired she could be after standing for hours in rubber boots that didn't fit well. She looked down. They were small and light and had slightly higher heels than the conventional ones, bought in an Oxford Street nurses' outfitters before she had been a theatre staff nurse. In theatres such as ENT and urological units where the floor was often awash with water, it was impossible to work wearing shoes, even if they were the obligatory white of the theatre shoes.

The first trolley was wheeled into the anaesthetic room and the sounds of steady breathing followed by the order to 'take him in', made everyone stand by his or her appointed task. The new sister watched carefully as her nurses positioned the man with his head slightly and comfortably raised. 'Mr Bill Grady,' she said, clearly, checked the name on the board with the notes and read the consent form.

'I checked,' said the anaesthetist. Rosalind saw a pair of light brown eyes looking at her over a mask that had slipped down and was covering only his mouth and not his nose.

'I'm sure you did,' said Rosalind, and smiled.

'I wondered what you'd be like, still don't know with you hidden in that lot.' The brown eyes were exploring her general contours and his glance rested on her boots. 'Not bad from the feet at any rate. Don't tell me that Beattie's issued you with decent boots?'

'All my own. I like to be comfortable,' she said and quickly glanced at the anaesthetic equipment, then turned away to see that the nurse scrubbed for the first case was correctly dressed and had everything she needed on the trolley. She could sense the gaze of the anaesthetist on her retreating form and vaguely resented it. His eyes had the glint of a womaniser and his cool appraisal of her fortunately shrouded figure told her that he had a very inflated opinion of himself and thought he was God's gift to women.

The first sterile towels were in position, leaving

only the mouth and nose of the patient revealed. The eyes were firmly hidden and protected by a towel applied almost like a turban and secured by figure-of-eight towel clips. A tube ran into Mr Grady's mouth and was connected to a laryngeal tube so that he could be anaesthetised without any hands having to interfere with the work to be done on his nose. Rosalind noticed that the tube was fixed neatly with sticking tape to one cheek and the cylinders on the apparatus were full. She smiled at the junior nurse, who was fairly new in the anaesthetic room, but obviously would be a good and reliable theatre nurse.

The operation went smoothly, the cartilage in the central dividing wall of the nose being gently resected from its covering mucous membrane, leaving a straighter septum and a greater channel for breathing. 'I'll do his sinuses while he's under,' said Mr Murray. A student who stood watching, wearing a white spectator's gown and mask, made a note and stood well back, looking very ill-at-ease.

'Your first Sub-Mucous Resection?' whispered Rosalind. He nodded and gulped. 'Don't worry. It gets a lot of people. Go out into my office for a breather, but come back for the next case.' He fled and Dr Alan King, the anaesthetist, laughed. 'I thought he's better out there than in here on the floor,' said Rosalind, tersely.

'True . . . very true. I hadn't noticed. Well done, Sister.' The calm pleasant voice of the surgeon cut across the growing tension. 'I remember my first mastoid. I just couldn't stand the crunch of bone and I passed clean out.'

'Is that why you began to take an interest in ENT?'

'You could say so . . . or you could say that it was the only branch of surgery that wasn't beyond me.'

'I don't believe that. ENT is a very specialised skill and takes endless patience.' It was ridiculous for him to make his work sound second-rate. Already, Rosalind could see that he was very good and wondered just how much of the general work was left to him to do. I suppose Mr Silk-tie-consultant Bradford swans off to do private cases and leaves everything to Mr Murray, she thought. As she went to fetch the next trolley, she saw the gaps in the instrument cupboard and glanced at the clock. It was still early and he would just be having breakfast, getting into his huge car or just reading his mail, she assumed. No way would he appear unless he had work to do that demanded an early start.

She was confused by her own unflattering opinion of the man she had seen only twice, only once at close quarters, and neither time being an occasion to be recalled with pleasure.

The floor was swabbed and gleaming as the next case came in. It was a simple case of nasal polyps and Tony Murray refused help. 'I can help myself to what I need if nurse will just hand me the washout at the end. No need to scrub.' This man had only a local anaesthetic and the whole operation took less time than it took to make sure that the inside of his nose was well and truly numbed with Lignocaine Hydrochlor gel. The junior nurse giggled and her hand shook as she tied a small nose bolster under the patient's nose, securing it by tapes tied on his head.

'You may laugh, Nurse,' said Tony Murray, 'But it catches all the drips and stops the patient from dabbing at the end of his nose with what seems to be invariably a grubby handkerchief.' Even the patient laughed as he was transferred from the table to the trolley. 'Let's hope we've got them all out this time,' said Mr Murray. 'But it didn't hurt, did it?' The patient tried to speak, but managed nothing more than a grunt and a weak smile. 'The numbness will soon wear off and you can go home tomorrow,' said Mr Murray.

The atmosphere was friendly and busy and the morning passed quickly. The last of the tonsillectomies was sent back to the children's ward and the list was over.

'You didn't need any anti-coagulant today,' said Rosalind.

'She bled a bit and I would have liked a note of her blood-clotting time, but she went back dry.' He frowned. 'I think I'll look in on my way down.'

'I'll go, Sir.' The student, now fully recovered from his attack of nausea, was eager to make up for his lapse. 'I can go now while you have coffee.'

'Fine . . . but I'll still look in later. What is the most dangerous time to watch?'

The theatre nurses gathered round to listen and the new sister believed that it was more important for them to have a valuable lecture than to get the theatre cleaned at once. 'When you dissect . . . I suppose. She went down dry, you said.'

'It's important to make sure there are no bleeding points oozing before letting a patient go back to the ward. Usually, as you saw, it is enough to sponge the face with very cold water as soon as you have turned the child on his side so that any blood and all the water run out rather than into his mouth and nose. When the water is clear and no further blood can be seen it's reasonable to think that all is well.' They looked at him in silence and Rosalind noticed that the junior anaesthetic nurse was absent, tidying her trolleys in the anaesthetic room, so she went to the door and told her to come and listen.

Dr Alan King was packing away his pen and notebook into a doctor's bag. He smiled and Rosalind saw that he was quite good looking now that he was neatly dressed. 'Not stopping for coffee?' she said, smiling, knowing that most men liked to relax for even a quick cup after a list.

'Not today. That's a pleasure I shall have soon, I hope.' It was a conventional reply, but said with a slight emphasis, as if the pleasure would be personal and not just the kind of friendly interlude between staff who worked well together. 'I have a private case to see and then an oesophagoscopy in St Cedric's Nursing Home.' He casually slipped a tube of lubricant jelly into his bag with a handful of new swabs and Rosalind was left with the impression that he was helping himself to hospital supplies.

She picked up a laryngoscope from the trolley and tested the light. It was bright and clean. She tested another and had the feeling that he was waiting for her to leave. A suspicion made her look at him closely. In the top pocket of his suit was a phial wrapped in gauze, opened with the top plugged with a rubber cork. 'Nice equipment here,' she said, lightly.

'Surely you'll leave that for the junior to put away?' he said.

'She's listening to a lecture on reactionary and secondary haemorrhage. She'll learn more from Mr Murray in five minutes than from an hour's study.' She lingered and polished the laryngoscope with a clean towel before placing it with the others in the glass cupboard. They lay in a neat row in varying sizes, making a set. They were all there. She closed the door and turned the key in the lock. The large laryngoscope that she had put back was not one that would be on the trolley for a list such as had been done that morning. It was more suitable for the first part of a trial insertion of a . . . large tube like an oesophagoscope?

'Don't let me keep you, as you are in a hurry,' she said sweetly, taking off her mask. The corners of her mouth twitched uncontrollably although her face was solemn. He saw the full and mobile lips trembling with pent-up humour and stared.

'I wish I could stay,' he said, in a low voice, forgetting that the new sister had foiled his attempt to borrow valuable hospital property, and remembering only red lips with mischief in the corners.

Rosalind went back to find the nurses busy and Tony Murray slipping off his theatre boots. He accepted the coffee brought to him and sipped it, gratefully. The central lights blazed down onto the theatre as gradually the chaos of soiled linen and bloody swabs was sorted out. Rosalind drank her coffee and excused herself, wanting to see where everything went after a case. She saw the flap that concealed the laundry shute and was told that bins went down in a small lift used by the theatre and the two wards along the corridor.

By the time she had changed her gown for her formal uniform, all traces of the morning's work had gone. 'Nice working with you, Sister,' called Tony Murray as he shrugged into his white coat. 'I'll just check that girl. Wasn't all that happy about her.' He frowned. 'What was her name?'

'Belinda Sykes.' He smiled and strode away, leaving the new sister feeling that if she could work with him during her time in the theatre at The Princess Beatrice Hospital, she would be content. A man with skill and good temper, no possibility of any romantic attachment because as he had told her only half an hour ago, he was married with two young children who he so obviously adored that there was no hint of him ever straying from the straight and narrow path of virtuous matrimony.

'He's very pleasant,' said Rosalind.

'A pet,' agreed Nurse Stephen. 'Not like Alan King!'

'No? He was very friendly.'

'Friendly . . . yes, you could say that,' she said, cryptically. 'Married, and in every department he talks of how unhappy he is and how his wife doesn't understand him.'

'Oh, like that? I shall harden my heart.'

'He's quite good fun if girls don't take him seriously. Sometimes I wonder if he is married. He

might be just saying it to have an escape route ready
after he finishes an affair.'

'It could be. I've met men like that, but if he's all
right at his work and with patients, I don't care if he
runs a harem.'

Nurse Stephen smiled. It would be interesting to
watch Alan try it on with the new sister. 'By the way
he eyed you, I'd say he would be hot on your trail
soon, Sister.'

'Rubbish. I think we might not be as friendly as
we were today if I catch him taking theatre equipment.'

Nurse Stephen laughed. 'You saw him take the
thio-pentone, did you?'

'How do you know? You weren't even on duty
during the first case.'

'Everyone knows Alan King. He is very plaus-
ible. After all, once a phial is opened, it is used and
the rest is thrown out and wasted. We never save
opened ampoules for the next list in case of con-
tamination. He argues that he is economising by
taking half a phial with him and using it up the same
morning on a private patient.'

'And charging the earth for his services?'

'Of course.' Nurse Stephen walked towards the
anaesthetic trolley. 'Good nurse . . . her first week
in theatre and shaping well.' She glanced at the
cupboard. 'I thought Alan was giving dope for an
oesophagoscopy?'

'So he said.'

'Well, Sister, either he has finally bought himself
some decent stuff, or you scared him off this morning.'

'I couldn't scare him.' Once more the twitch of hidden mirth lurked at the corners of her mouth.

'Oh, Sister! I think you knew all the time that he might take the laryngoscope.'

'I had one rocket yesterday about the fenestration instruments, so I'm glad I didn't have to put my convictions to the test again,' said Rosalind with feeling.

'May I go to lunch, Sister?'

'Is it so late? Of course. We have two biopsies of nodules this afternoon. Can you take them? No anaesthetic except for a spray. They can be done in the anaesthetic room as outpatients.'

'That's what we have been doing. It's nice to know that you agree with most of our routine, Sister.' They smiled and Rosalind had a warm feeling that she could have a very happy time with the staff she had at present.

'Off to lunch with you and I'll go off duty from second lunch. Has the list come for tomorrow? If it's not on my desk, could you fetch it on your way back? I'd like to see it before I go off.'

'I'll pick it up. By the way, Sister, I've left the notes on surgeons on your desk.'

Rosalind sat at the smart new light wood desk and opened the well-thumbed notebook. She had hoped that Beattie's followed the custom of having such a book in each theatre, with all the likes and dislikes of each surgeon written clearly so that even a nurse who had never seen one of the surgeons could lay up a trolley for him with everything he preferred to use ready for his case. She smiled at some of the entries. Some notes were more than frank about less popular surgeons, but as the book was compiled by many different nurses and sisters, it was impossible to lay the blame for any entry at any particular door. She became absorbed, suddenly seeing the range of operations done in her theatre. She knew of the research done over the years and the good results that surgeons from Beattie's had achieved, but she was not familiar with all the details of the arrangements necessary for items used during the operations.

She sighed. If only the one cloud on her career would vanish, she could be happy, but she glanced again and again at the spaces in the instrument cupboard and wondered when the forceful, rude and completely overbearing man would return them. She returned to the book and the corners of her mouth twitched yet again. Someone had drawn a cartoon in the back of the book of a team of surgeons huddled together as if they were in a rugby scrum, the only difference being that they were bent over a microscope. She heard a movement from the door and looked across the room. A shadow receded and a man walked into the instrument room.

Sister Rosalind Mason straightened the bow under her chin and walked out of her office. At least he might have the courtesy to make some remark as he entered her small domain! Annoyance lent her courage as she stood by the door and watched him go into the theatre, leaving his bag on a trolley. 'NURSE! . . . Nurse Stephen,' he called.

'Can I help you?' Her voice was cold. 'It might be

easier if you ask me about my staff. Or couldn't you see me sitting in my office?' As the office had a wall that was half glazed, it was clear that nobody could pass without seeing who was seated at the desk.

'I wanted Nurse Stephen.'

'And I could have told you where she is. At lunch, as it happens.' He looked down at the bag and at the drums left by a porter who had followed him. Rosalind continued to stand quite still, making no movement or sign to show that she noticed the case.

'I wanted her to unpack for me.' He glared at her as if she was responsible for the absence of the staff nurse.

'She'll be back from lunch in half an hour,' she said. 'If there is nothing else you want, Mr Bradford, please excuse me. I was in the middle of checking on all the requirements and . . . idiosyncrasies of the various surgeons.' His face was stern but under his enigmatic brows was a glint of fire, of something other than anger but not as warm as laughter. 'I'm learning a lot about this theatre.' Her lips twitched and she hid the smile in her eyes so that he saw the long curling eyelashes against the soft peach bloom of her cheeks.

With a sense of triumph, she left him with his case and the used and empty dressing drums. I will *not* wait on him when it has nothing to do with this theatre, she thought. But she heard him go into the anaesthetic room and try the locked door of the cupboard there. What does he want now? Footsteps came back and she bent over the book as if absorbed.

'Sister?' The word was forced from his lips.

'Mr Bradford?'

'Have you the keys to the cupboard?'

'Which one?' she asked, innocently.

'The one in there.' He waved a hand vaguely in the direction of the theatre. She stood up and went towards him, her bunch of keys in her hand.

'Just give me the keys. I can see that you are busy.'

'It's no trouble, Mr Bradford. Tell me what you wish to see.'

'I need to borrow the dilators for a patient downstairs,' he said. 'He *is* a patient here . . . they will *not* leave the hospital and I take full responsibility for them.' The sarcasm was biting, the deep-set eyes cold. 'I have to use these as they are the only set in the hospital. Satisfied, Sister?'

'Of course, Mr Bradford. If I know where our equipment is being used and check it out and back again, there is no problem if it is being used within the hospital.' She unlocked the cupboard door and took out the long velvet-lined box containing a graduated set of metal beads on the ends of long thin steel wires, together with what looked like a string of metal beads on strong nylon. These also were graduated. Rosalind opened the box to make sure that the set was complete and as she did so, the fabric hinge that was already badly frayed with age, parted company with the heavier box.

As she grabbed at it to save the contents falling, the string of metal beads sprang out and scattered over the floor. Two heads bent low to retrieve the rolling beads and two heads crashed into each other. 'Hell!' said the consultant, shaking his head. Rosalind sat heavily on the floor. 'Let me help you up.' This time, the glint was maliciously amused.

'I can manage,' she said, scrambling up, but her foot found one of the beads and she slid across the floor, clutching wildly at something—anything with which to save herself from falling again.

'I said I'd help you.' Strong arms held her in an iron grip, firm hands that were strangely gentle, strangely . . . safe, and as she looked up, startled, his eyes were suddenly devoid of any expression. She was aware of a slight pain where the watch she wore pinned to her breast pocket had dug into the soft flesh under her uniform as he held her in that sudden tight embrace for . . . was it only a second?

They picked up the beads and Rosalind checked them against the depressions into which they fitted. 'Why do you want them?' she said, to ease the tension.

'A man broke into a house to burgle it and drank what he thought was wine.' He looked sombre. 'He had to telephone the police and give himself up. They rushed him here and found he'd drunk acid by mistake.' Rosalind shuddered. 'He was in a bad way and we had to put in a gastrostomy tube and feed him like that while his oesophagus healed. He is still full of contracted tissue, but we dilate the external tube end with these and keep the oesophagus dilated by a weighted rubber catheter which he swallows at intervals.'

'I've heard it was done but never seen it. How on earth do you get him to swallow the catheter?' Her interest made her forget her embarrassment.

He laughed—for the first time—and it was as if the sun came out over a troubled sea and dazzled everyone with its brightness. He smoothed down the wings of dark hair that were tinged with grey, and actually laughed. 'He sits with a newspaper for half an hour, reading with a damn great bougie down his throat as if he is digesting it. He is no longer frightened to swallow it and doesn't even react when it is removed.' He closed the box. 'He's a hard case, but he has courage. I hope he keeps out of trouble when he leaves here.'

'Was he charged? For the burglary?'

'No. I think the householders felt guilty about putting acid into a wine bottle and not labelling it. They could have found their own children drinking it—a sobering thought.' He glanced at her with a hint of amusement and once more, the new sister had to remind herself that she had a certain status. Why could he make her feel ten inches high by just a glance?

She locked the cupboard again and put the keys into her dress pocket. 'Is that all you need? I expect they have lubricant and lotions on the ward?' She glanced at the anaesthetic trolley and her practised eye told her that something was missing. Alan King *had* taken the tube of water-soluble lubricant that should have been on the trolley ready to make the instruments such as airways and laryngoscopes smooth and slippery as they were eased into place into sensitive throats.

Mr Bradford saw where she was looking. 'Alan King been borrowing again?' He looked annoyed. He swung round to the main cupboard and saw the neat line of laryngoscopes, the angled metal with tiny lights attached with which one can examine the back of throats and into the larynx or voice box. 'You never let him take those!' It was an order made in the voice she had once thought was the only one that this strange cold man used.

'He hasn't asked me for them,' she said.

'It's against the rules and dangerous for essential instruments to be away from here when they might be needed in a hurry.'

She raised her eyebrows. 'I repeat, Mr Bradford, he hasn't asked me for them and I think I can handle the situation should it arise.'

He glared at her as if suspecting some discourtesy, but she stood slim and tall and cool although her heart was beating fast. I mustn't let him see that he scares me. I have to work here with him . . . heaven help me and if he thinks I'm just a door mat, I shall have a terrible time.

'I hope you can,' he said.

'I think I can hear the lift,' she said. 'That might be Nurse Stephen back from lunch.' In spite of her cold hands and inward agitation, she appeared calm. 'I'll call her and you can give her your . . . orders, Sir.' She walked steadily away, her slim hips defiant. She turned and paused, the lips mobile again with repressed laughter. 'I hope that your needs don't take too much of her time, Mr Bradford. She will have to pack the drums, the hospital drums, to make sure they are where they should be—in the theatre when needed.'

'If you look carefully, Sister, you will see my name on each of those drums. I merely have them filled and sterilised here.' He frowned and stalked into the office where Nurse Stephen was looking at the operation list for the next day. He looked over her shoulder, and gave a short, humourless laugh. 'I see we have the oto-sclerosis tomorrow. I take it that you will be scrubbing for me, Nurse Stephen?'

Rosalind froze. He had put her neatly in the wrong again and had shown her staff nurse that he had no opinion of the new sister in his theatre. 'I'm going to lunch now, Nurse Stephen,' she said.

He turned and nodded, as if dismissing her. 'If you can spare a few minutes, Nurse, it would save time tomorrow.' He was deliberately excluding the girl in the green iniform. He placed his body so that his back hid the nurse from the doorway and he spoke in low tones about the dressings he wanted to try for the case first on the next day's list.

Biting her lip, Rosalind walked away from the theatre unit. I hate it here, she thought. I detest him and everything he stands for. I was mad to come and think I could find a place among people like him. They aren't my kind and I should have known it. Where was her dream of working in a world-famous hospital? Where was the dream that she had dreamt as a girl of being with the very best . . . working and finding fulfilment with the greatest surgeons in the world? She had heard so much of the miracles of surgery that happened at Beattie's and hospitals like her, she had heard tales of the dedication and effort that went into every case, every contact. Her heart was heavy with humiliation as she went into the dining room.

'You look peaky . . . have a busy morning?'

Sister Wendy Fletcher saw the strain and unshed tears. 'Buck up . . . he gives everyone hell at first.'

'But I haven't even scrubbed for him yet and we've had two rows already!'

'Don't hate him too much on sight.' Wendy laughed. 'You know what they say? Hate is akin to love . . . you might go overboard for him and that would never do, would it?'

'Could anyone even *like* a cold fish like him?'

'Cold? You have to be joking. Even steel can burn.' She sighed and refused pudding. 'I'll have lots of coffee and then I can convince myself I'm not hungry,' she said. 'Have to slim before Easter. Got a date.'

'Lucky you,' said Rosalind. 'I've gone off men.'

CHAPTER THREE

GRADUALLY, it was all coming back. The new theatre sister wandered down the drive to post letters and to buy stamps and ask for the local edition of what was on in London in March. I might as well get used to living in a big city again, she thought. It would be good to line up a few outings to take her mind off work. But she knew that she needed no change as yet and would find all her pleasure and excitement in her very own theatre, if it weren't for one cloud on a breathlessly clear horizon . . .

'You'll be the new sister, Sister,' Claud grinned. 'Never forget a face, but you weren't here for long, were you?' He rooted in a tin box for the stamps she wanted and found a few leaflets on local places of interest. 'Turning me into a blooming travel agency, they are,' he said.

She stuck the stamps to the envelopes and slipped the letters into the box. There were so few people who would be really interested in her work. Her aunt was far away and the two cousins only kept in touch at Christmas and birthdays. She knew that the girls with whom she had trained were still nursing, but scattered so far wide and moving from job to job so that they could see the world, that it was difficult to catch up with them. She hoped her letter to Maureen who was working in Saudi Arabia would get there safely. She must be very lonely at times in a country with different customs, great restrictions and none of her own friends or family with whom she could laugh or grumble.

But it was her own loneliness that made her think of Maureen. Why lonely? How could any girl be sad when she had been given a plum post in a famous hospital to do the work for which she had been trained? And I *have* been trained and I can do whatever is needed in there even if he tries to reduce me to a quivering jelly, she told herself. She tossed her head and walked back to the Nurses' Home, going by way of the side paths that lay near the outer walls, under the slight misting of green in the tall poplars and the first buds of the ornamental cherry trees. She came to the terrace—or what was left of it after half had been used for the new block. The tennis courts were still there beyond a high laurel hedge. Her spirits rose. Wendy Fletcher had mentioned that she played. She went to her room and found some white shorts and a pale yellow shirt.

Being virtually alone, except for the aunt who she visited whenever she was on holiday or between jobs or training sessions, it was vital to travel light as she had to take everything she possessed with her when rooms had to be cleared to make room for others in her absence. It also meant that Rosalind had everything she needed and never sent urgent messages to relatives for tennis shoes, warm skirts when the weather changed or bikinis when the water beckoned. She shook the creases from the shirt and took it down to press it with other garments that had suffered in the suitcase. I'll have to buy a new racquet and tennis balls if they don't supply them, she thought. She made a mental note to look for them when next she had a day off.

She heard sounds of nurses passing the kitchen door and was pleased when Sister Wendy Fletcher burst in. 'Thought you'd be here. After you with the iron. I brought some buns back and I can iron and have tea at the same time. What's that? Shorts? Oh, now I'll have to play. I need someone like you to make me hop about a bit. I'll just put the kettle on and get my own kit. I could do with some new shorts.'

Rosalind smiled. There wasn't time to say a word when Wendy got wound up. She finished pressing a deep blue skirt and hung the pale blue finely-ribbed velvet shirt in the steam from the kettle to ease out the creases. It would do if there was any hospital entertainment like a music club, film shows, whatever they had, if anything. 'Any social life here?' she asked.

'Not a lot,' said Wendy. 'So many of the staff live out that it's difficult, but we do have a thriving music society that takes in all kinds so that nobody is bored by a diet of pure Wagner or pop. A few dances, tennis and badminton and, of course, trips to our very own local, the Falcon.'

'I remember. I went there a couple of times, but we were all so exhausted when we were doing midder that nothing made much impression on me.'

'Oh, you must go to the Falcon, with a boss like yours, how can you stay away?'

Rosalind distrusted the wicked smile. 'What do you mean?' she asked, cautiously. 'He doesn't own that, too?'

'No, but there are bars and eating places there named after birds of prey.'

'So . . . he's a bird watcher?'

Wendy laughed. 'That's what he's *not*, or not as in dolly bird.'

'Do you always talk in riddles?'

'Most of the time,' said Wendy, cheerfully. 'You get like that after being in charge of kids' ward. But didn't you know? Mr Bradford is called Peregrine, and come to think of it, he's rather like one.'

'He has a nasty spiteful beak and a very unfriendly eye, but there the similarity ends,' said Rosalind. 'Peregrines are beautiful, dignified, proud and free.'

'That's Sir to a T.'

'No, that's not true. I meant the bird.'

'Well, you seem to have ruffled each other's feathers. You'll get used to him. He is a very reserved man, not unfeeling.' Wendy was serious. 'You'll have to talk to Anna. Her husband—I think I told you about them—she is Sister orthopaedic theatre and he is the gynae. consultant.' Rosalind nodded. 'They know more about Peregrine Bradford than anyone here. He was a friend of Slade's back in their first MB days. I think there was some tragedy way back that made him a bit sombre.'

'Has he a family? Surely his wife . . .'

'His wife? You have to be joking.' Wendy glanced at the new sister sharply. Hadn't she asked that question before when they mentioned him?

She was trying not to appear interested in him as a person, but leading Wendy on to talk about him. 'I think he had a love affair which went wrong or she died . . . I don't know the details. He has a hide-away in the country to which he disappears without trace from time to time. I think Anna and Slade know all about it, but they don't discuss him in that way.' She folded her freshly ironed dress and began on her tennis things. 'We could play this weekend if you like. I'm on call and have to be here at the end of a phone, but I can play on Sunday if the sky doesn't fall.'

'Sunday afternoon would be great. I'll look forward to it. I'll make the tea. This is much nicer than the dining room.'

'You're learning. This old kitchen can tell some tales. It's been the scene for all kinds of drama— Love, hate, sorrow and just about everything has happened here.'

'Everything?'

'Well, not quite, it's a bit public for more than tea and sympathy.'

'Are you on duty tonight? I'm back at five to give Nurse Stephen another break. She had a tough time last month when they were short-staffed and the last sister left early. Why *did* she leave? Nobody ever told me.'

'She didn't get on with . . . people. She wasn't Beattie's-trained and she rubbed everyone up the wrong way.'

Rosalind licked her dry lips. 'I'm not Beattie's-trained,' she said. 'And I haven't exactly made the perfect start with certain people.'

'More tea please, and don't worry. I've heard what the nurses think on the grapevine and you'll do.'

'You mean it? The nurses think I'm OK?'

'I told you . . . and not only the nurses.'

'Well, everyone must get on well with Mr Murray. I can't imagine him upsetting anyone.'

'He's not the only one you have to please to survive.'

Rosalind had a vision of a dark handsome head with soft wings of hair and shaggy eyebrows. 'No,' she said, sadly. 'Others might be more difficult to please.'

As they climbed the stairs to their rooms, the telephone rang and they heard someone answering it. 'Sister Fletcher?'

'Here!' shouted Wendy. She pushed her bundle of clothes into Rosalind's arms on top of her own pile. 'Pop them in my room would you? I'd better answer it. I have a feeling it might be trouble.' She ran down the stairs after the girl who had called her. Rosalind went up to put the clothes on Wendy's bed and then to her own room. She put the clothes away in the cupboard and drawers and left the room looking neat and inviting, with her personal touches to make it seem a real home. A set of miniatures left to her by her grandmother were on one wall and in a delicate Wedgwood bowl were early daffodils. She straightened two figurines of London street cries and picked up her cloak again.

Before she could reach Wendy's room to go with her on duty, the other sister came panting up the stairs. 'Have to run . . . I almost expected it. That tonsil, it's bleeding. I thought she was swallowing when I left the ward and put a special to watch her. I'd better go and check.'

'And I'll put in a set just in case,' called Rosalind. They hurried across to the main new building and for once, the lift was waiting on the ground floor. Wendy almost ran from the lift and Rosalind went on up to the theatre floor.

'You're back early, Sister.' Staff Nurse Stephen smiled. 'A quiet afternoon and I've done most of the prep. for tomorrow. Should be quite a morning.'

'Never mind that now,' Rosalind said, crisply. 'Sister Fletcher thinks the red-head this morning might be bleeding. Put a dissection set in to boil and I'll lay up a trolley. It might be a false alarm, but we must be ready.' She took off her cap and cuffs and covered her uniform with a voluminous white gown. She tied the tapes of a mask over the green cap and began to lay up a sterile trolley. 'Nurse!' she called and the junior came running. 'Bleep Dr King, find out if he's in the building. Ask him to contact us. And Nurse . . . do the same for Mr Murray. If we're needed, we shall have to be organised.'

In a few minutes, the trolley was ready, the bins out and the scrubbing bay prepared. Rosalind checked the cylinders and the monitors and made sure that the intravenous fluids that might be required were ready, with a cutting-down set for use if a patient was badly collapsed and a needle couldn't find the vein. She thought back to the morning. The girl had her tonsils dissected, but Mr

Murray had left her adenoids. Years ago, every child who came to theatre had adenoids removed as routine when they came in for removal of tonsils. Fashions change and Mr Murray believed in leaving any that weren't full of infection as they were lymphoid glands that helped, with healthy tonsils, to protect the body from infection spreading from the mouth and nose to the blood stream. When they were all grossly infected, however, they were an added risk and their removal was necessary. In this case, Belinda was lucky that her adenoids were not enlarged and Tony Murray had wondered if they had been curetted when she was an infant.

The telephone rang. 'Alan King here.'

'Oh, Dr King, I thought you ought to know that Belinda Sykes is giving cause for concern. Sister Fletcher has gone back to the ward and I have laid a trolley in case the child has to come back to the theatre.'

'Damn, I was on my way out to play golf. Just my luck,' he sounded sorrowful and Rosalind almost wanted to say how much she understood and how hard it was for him, when she recalled what she had heard about him. He should be on duty, not swanning off to play golf! He had some light anaesthetics to give in Major Casualty during the evening session and there just wasn't time for him to go out to a golf course. Rosalind smiled. He was playing for sympathy as Wendy and Nurse Stephen had said he would.

'Hard cheese. We all have to suffer. I had the theatre aseptic for tomorrow and now we might have it bloodied up again.' She heard him sigh.

'Where can I contact you if she comes to theatre?'

'I'll be in Cas. Major,' he said. 'Is Tony around? I rather thought he had a family birthday today or some such irresistible festivity.' He sounded bored. 'I keep away from such occasions as much as possible, but he laps it up.'

'You mean he isn't available? Who takes his place on call?'

'His HS, but he isn't all that experienced. He's fine for doling out the odd medication, but this might be rough.' At last he sounded concerned. 'Leave it to me. I'll pop down to the ward and check . . . there's no point in raising a full team unless we're needed. I'll check and let you know if the child is bleeding and then get someone to cope.'

'Thank you . . . I'm very grateful.'

'I hope so,' he said, and his voice purred as if he contemplated a treat in the future. She put down the telephone. The junior nurse was cleaning the glass inside the spectators' gallery window and the screen of the video. At least most of the students now sat away from the action and watched the procedures on the screen. She checked that there was an ampoule of Menaphthone ready and was glad that Sister Fletcher's parting remark was to tell her that they used that preparation of synthetic Vitamin K, a powerful drug to stop bleeding, rather than any of the other preparations. She made a note in the book that the drug was now in current use in the childrens' ward.

'When the child comes up, if she does, tell me at once what drugs she has had in the ward. I shall write them on the board so that there is no danger of the anaesthetist or any other person giving more by mistake. If we are busy, it could happen that an order is given and two people think they are responsible. Bring any drugs you are told to use to me for checking, however busy you think I am. If there is any doubt, I can ask the surgeon.' The clock hands slunk past the hour and the telephone rang sharply again.

'Fletcher here. She's been swallowing regularly and is beginning to look pale. She's conscious now and what is coming away is going into her stomach. I think she's losing fast. She's had intra-muscular Vit K. You have some there if we need more?'

'Yes ... I have the type you mentioned. Menaphthone.' Rosalind glanced at the clock. 'You should bring her up if she hasn't stopped swallowing blood in five minutes.'

'That's right. I've seen Alan and he is ready.'

'Has he contacted someone to do it? Mr Murray isn't in the building.'

'All laid on, just get the trolley ready and the sucker going. He may want a stomach tube to take away the blood in case she's sick and makes her throat bleed again after it's stopped.'

'It's all there. I'll get nurse scrubbed up.' She turned from the telephone and heard the sound of water gushing in the scrubbing bay. Good, she thought. Nurse Stephen is leaving nothing to chance. She went into the bay to open the sterile drum in which the surgical gloves were kept, adjusting her mask before entering the theatre proper. There were two figures at the sinks. Nurse Stephen was drying her hands on a sterile towel

handed to her by the junior nurse on the end of
forceps, and a man in theatre green and huge white
boots was turning away from the sink with dripping
hands, waiting for a towel. 'Go into the anaesthetic
room, Nurse, and tell them to bring her straight in
on the table in case we have to tilt her quickly,'
Rosalind said. She picked up a sterile towel on the
end of the long forceps and handed it to the man.
Her heart sounded as if everyone must hear it
beating, as she watched Mr Peregrine Bradford dry
his hands and reach for the packet of gloves. She
watched him powder his hands with the special
talc-free powder and draw on first one glove and
then the other. He flexed his hands and she was
absurdly relieved that his gloves were sound and
new. A split glove at a time like this would be
disastrous to his temper.

'Thank you, Nurse,' he said. She blushed under
her mask. Either he mistook her for someone, was
absent-minded, or was refusing to consider her the
new sister in charge of the theatre unit. But there
was no time for such conjecture. The lift whined,
the trolley was pushed into the theatre, and the
child lifted on to the table quickly. Alan King was
dripping chloroform slowly on to a padded face
mask as he came into the theatre, and already the
child was asleep.

'Let's hope that's enough,' said Mr Bradford.
'I'll be as quick as I can.' He reached for the
Boyle-Davis gag and opened the mouth of the
lifeless-looking child. Rosalind was shocked. She
had lost a great deal of blood and it was only due to
the vigilance of the skilled nursing staff that it had

been noticed so soon. No blood appeared on the outside and it was only the deep, compulsive swallowing that had indicated the true state of affairs.

Nurse Stephen handed over the long swab forceps in which were securely fastened the gauze swabs that wiped away the blood and left the site of operation clear. The light from the surgeon's headlamp gleamed bright and showed one small bleeding point oozing rapidly. 'Suture.' And Nurse Stephen handed him a curved needle threaded with silk thread on the end of a long needle holder. 'Good. I think I'd better anchor the ligature in case it slips.' He tied off the bleeding point and sat looking down into the pink cavern. One after another, he used swabs and discarded them, watching closely for other signs of bleeding. 'We have a slight ooze here. Not even a blood vessel I can tie.' He glanced up at the nonchalant figure at the head of the table. 'I can't use Adrenalin if you use that stuff. Can't you switch?'

'I didn't think you'd be as long as this,' said Alan King, sulkily. 'You could use a little . . . she wouldn't absorb much.'

'Rubbish' The voice had the cold edge that Rosalind thought was reserved only for her. 'It's asking for trouble. You know there have been cases when inexperienced men have mixed chloroform or Trichloroethylene with Adrenalin therapy and had near tragedies on their hands. It's never going to happen in *my* theatre.' He waved a hand in the air. 'What else can we use? Sister? What do you think?'

'She's had a full dose of Vit. K which should take effect before she leaves here. We have glucose . . .

old-fashioned but they used to use it when they
used chloroform masks more for T's and A's.'
Rosalind went to the cupboard and brought the
sticky solution which she poured into a galley pot.
He will now tell me I'm a senseless idiot and throw a
fit, she thought. She stood by the head of the table,
watching as he dipped a swab into the glucose
solution and applied it to the oozing tissue. He
grunted, as if reserving judgment. He held the swab
in position for what seemed like minutes and then
drew it away. No further oozing occurred and
Rosalind breathed more easily.

'Brilliant,' said a mildly sarcastic voice from the
badly-worn masked face of the anaesthetist. 'Have
you a supply of viper venom too, Sister?' He
laughed. 'Or what else could we use? Throw the
bones and examine the entrails of a chicken? Use
the coagulem that went out of fashion twenty years
ago?'

Rosalind fumed, silently. The swine! He was
trying to take the fire from his own lack of fore-
thought by making fun of her, knowing that Mr
Bradford would share his views.

The quiet voice was icy and cut through the
fatuous laughter. 'Russell Viper venom is still used
in many instances when other drugs can not be
used. Adrenalin would have been good, but on
second thoughts this is better as it doesn't raise the
blood pressure and so give rise to further bleeding
when the initial effect has worn off.' He nodded
curtly in the direction of Rosalind who stood rooted
to the spot in incredulous wonder. 'Thank you,
Sister. I think she'll do.'

'Are you going to wash out her stomach?'

'No. Sister Fletcher said she was sick before she came to the theatre. We were right to bring her back. I saw just how much she lost. You can stop anaesthetising the whole theatre with that stuff.' Mr Bradford gently removed the gag that had kept the mouth open wide during the investigation. He wiped the pale face with a damp swab and listened to her stertorous breathing. 'Take her pulse, Sister, and ask Sister to keep up a half-hourly chart for three hours.' He glanced at the board where Rosalind had noted the times and amounts of the medicaments given to the child before she reached the theatre. He nodded approval. 'I like that . . . it saves time and any danger of mix-ups. Did you learn that where you trained?'

'No.' She bit her lip, unwilling to tell him, but he stood looking at her, thoughtfully. 'I learned it here on the midwifery block,' she said.

He laughed and the laughter showed above his mask. 'So you've found that Beattie's can do some things well?'

'I've never doubted it or I wouldn't have come back.'

'True, but I had a feeling that you might be regretting it.'

The trolley was gone, with the junior nurse holding the intravenous bottle aloft—already, the colour was coming back into Belinda's cheeks, and the drip was set to run slowly.

'The clotting time wasn't checked before she was admitted,' said Rosalind, resolutely ignoring his comments about her attitude to the hospital.

'Shouldn't they have tests before T's and A's?'

'You are very quick, Sister, and right again—this time.' He frowned and she wondered what he was going to say to spoil it. What hadn't she done that was making him look like that? As if he knew what she was thinking, a slow smile spread over his face. 'You aren't very quick with coffee.'

'Oh! Nurse, did you put any coffee on?' She knew the answer—everyone had forgotten. 'I'm sorry, Mr Bradford, I think we've let you down.' She took off her mask.

'All right,' he said, coolly. 'Don't look as if I'm going to bite you. I can have dinner at the Falcon.' He looked round the wet and gown-strewn floor. 'But you have a lot to do if the theatre is to be immaculate for my list at eight-thirty tomorrow morning.'

'Eight-thirty? I thought it was an hour later.'

'I have other work to do later. Of course, if you can't manage it . . .' He regarded her with a sardonic lift to his eyebrows.

'Of course we can . . . if we are told what time the cases are expected. I hope the wards know when to give their pre-medication drugs?'

She had the satisfaction of seeing his face darken and he looked away. Alan King came back from the ward.

'Eight-thirty all right for you tomorrow, Alan?'

The anaesthetist lost his wary expression and smiled. 'Fine,' said Mr Peregrine Bradford. He rubbed his hands together as if well satisfied and left the theatre with an almost affable nod to the two people left staring after him.

'The old devil! I came back expecting a rocket because I didn't take the right course and he knew it. He deliberately let me go to the ward thinking he was furious. I was rehearsing all my excuses on the way back and then, wham! He was as nice as pie just to throw me . . . and get his own way. He knows I hate getting up and coming in at some unearthly hour. He also knows that Matron doesn't approve of cases as big as the ones tomorrow starting too early as it rushes the day staff.'

'Rushes isn't the word! I shall have to come on duty before breakfast to see that everything is humming and then have breakfast and come on duty again. If it was a ward it wouldn't be so bad, but it means changing twice more. Is he like this all the time?'

'All the time,' said Alan King, calmly and with obvious satisfaction. 'You and I will just have to form an . . . alliance and fight him together.' He was suddenly close to her and she moved away. He looked at his watch. 'I suppose I ought to grab some food, too, but I shall make sure it's in another part of the local. I couldn't stand talking shop with our brilliant surgeon tonight.'

'And as he said, I have work to do. See you tomorrow.' Rosalind went into the sterilising room with her staff nurse. Even if Mr Peregrine Bradford was the original male chauvinist pig, she had no desire to join forces with Alan King under any pretext. 'You do the theatre and I'll do the instruments,' she said. 'Nurse, you go to supper and do the sluicing when you come back.'

'You should go down now, Sister. I'm non-

resident and live in the hostel on the hill and we've
got food in for tonight after duty . . . if that's all
right?'

'I'm not hungry, I'll get a snack later, too. I want
to get as much done for the morning as we can. Did
you know the list has been changed for an hour
earlier?'

Nurse Stephen gasped. 'But Matron will be livid!
Even Mr Bradford knows that he's going a bit far to
expect that. I shall have to be up at dawn!'

'If we get organised now, you needn't come in
any earlier. You'll need all your beauty sleep if you
are to scrub for two long cases.'

'You want me to?'

'Yes, I think I'd prefer to watch this time. I can
cope with the microscope. Fortunately, I had some
experience with micro-surgery in the accident wing
in my last theatre.'

'Fingers and toes being sewn on are a bit different from this delicate stuff.'

'Not really. The blood vessels have to be sewn
together and the nerves put into apposition. The
apparatus is the same at all events.' She looked at
the clock. 'You've been an angel. Go off now and I
won't forget that you haven't had any real off duty
today; make it up at the weekend.'

Nurse Stephen brightened. 'If I could have a half
day before my day off, I could go home.' She
finished putting out all the unsterile things needed
for the next day and fled, 'Before anything else
comes in!'

It was fairly late when Sister Rosalind Mason
went off duty. The theatre looked good and poised

for action and she wasn't altogether displeased with the way the evening had gone. He had actually approved of something she had suggested. She hugged her cloak round her and went out into the blustery drive. The air was good after the air-conditioning of her department and she paused, taking long, deep breaths. She saw Sister Fletcher emerge from the hospital block and hurried after her.

'Just off duty? So am I. That young woman threshed about a bit . . . don't like Alan's efforts with a drip bottle. How is it? Ready for tomorrow?'

'Which question do you like answered first? You shoot them at me like bullets.'

'It's being on kids,' said Wendy, cheerfully. 'I ought to have known with a name like mine that I'd end up in Never-Never Land. The children shout at me and I shout back just to get a word in edgewise.'

Rosalind smiled. She had heard that Sister Wendy Fletcher was a very good sister who stood no nonsense but managed her ward with humour and love. 'We start at dawn tomorrow, or some of us do. Mr Bossman will wander in at eight-thirty ready to scrub and we shall have been up for hours getting ready for him.'

'Eight-thirty? That's a bit steep now that so many of the staff live out. What's on?'

'One stapedectomy, one fenestration and a cold mastoid.'

'All fairly long ops?'

'I don't know. Some surgeons take hours and some seem to have got the technique down to the minimum. Having not seen Mr Bradford in action except for the tiny thing today, I can't judge his ability.'

'Well, that's fair anyhow. I thought you disliked him so much that you'd condemn him in every sphere.' They reached the Nurses' Home. I'm hungry. Did you get any supper? I had one biscuit and a cup of coffee on the ward. I'm starving!'

'I wasn't hungry enough to go down and I had tomorrow's list on my mind so I missed it too. What can we have?'

'We could change and wander over to the Falcon. They do a very good toasted sandwich and nice pies.'

'Not the Falcon,' said Rosalind, hastily.

'No? Have you heard that they make their meat pies from stray cats or something?'

'No . . . but I think the place will be lousy with men from here. I know that Mr Bradford is having dinner there and Dr King is going there, too, although he did say he would avoid Mr Bradford if possible.'

'Mr Bradford will be in the restaurant—can you imagine him coming down to our level to eat toasted sandwiches?' They giggled and Rosalind decided that the way to think of her intimidating boss was to laugh at him, if possible. 'And Alan will be in the bar. That leaves at least two places where we can eat.'

'I'm feeling much too fragile to risk an encounter with either of them tonight. You haven't had the doubtful pleasure of their company during the past few hours.'

'I wouldn't have thought you'd be scared of them.'

'I'm not, certainly not of Alan King. He's a bit of a pain in the neck and the less I see of him, the better.'

'He's all right if he knows he can't flannel his way through your department. Been borrowing yet, has he?' Rosalind nodded, and told her that it was nothing more than a couple of expendables from the trolley. 'Let him know that you'll have no nonsense and he'll be fine. He's a coward at heart . . . aren't we all? Well, if you can't face them, at least let's change and wander along to that new fish and chipper down the road. Join the queue of skinheads and walk back smelling strongly of fish and acetic acid.'

'Is it good?'

'I've tried it once and it was super. Come on, get that uniform off and we'll hit the town.'

Rosalind slipped out of her green dress and shook her hair free. It felt good to let the air flow through the thick honey-coloured strands, to lift it with a brush and send it down her back in a spiral of gold. She dashed on a bright lipstick and buttoned a thick woollen coat of crimson over a turquoise shirt and skirt, dragged on crimson ribbed stockings and caught up a shiny black hand bag to match the high-heeled shoes. She met Wendy in the corridor, snuggly wrapped in a long fake fur coat that made her sweet plump face look soft and feminine. 'You look too smart for the local chipper,' said Rosalind.

'Speak for yourself. It doesn't matter, the locals seem to know who is from the hospital and we never have trouble. It's more likely that I shall have to listen to the life history of a former patient while we move up in the queue.' She looked at Rosalind. 'Now, you, you're lucky. You could stand out there for hours with every member of staff passing you by and not be recognised. That hair makes you look another girl. Very handy. I stick out as that sister on children's, whatever I wear.'

'It has been useful sometimes,' said Rosalind, 'and I haven't been here long enough for people to get to know my other self.'

They walked down through the dark drive and out between the high wrought-iron gates that had never been shut since Wendy came to Beattie's. 'It would take an invasion to make them shut them now, but I love them. I like to pause when I come back after a day off and see the moon shining through the sort of filigree the wrought iron makes at the top of the gates. It's like coming back to the old country mansion. It's certainly like coming home. You'll feel it too, when you've been here for a few weeks.'

'If everyone was like you and Mr Murray, I'd be at home now.' She stared at the outline of the theatre block, high above the road and now in darkness. 'I wonder if I shall ever get on with Mr Bradford?' It was a wistful question, and she couldn't think why it was important that he should think well of her. Other places, other people had been not all she could want, but she had been able to shrug away events that annoyed or irritated her and make the best of the ones that pleased her. She thought of the firm hands that gently washed the face of the child on the operating table. He'd be wonderful with children, she thought, with a sense of shocked discovery.

The chip shop was brightly lit and as Wendy said, everyone passing could see who was queuing for cod and chips. 'I'll fool them and have plaice,' she said, then sighed. 'Wait for it,' she said from the corner of her mouth.

'Well, if it isn't Sister Fletcher,' said a voice, and Rosalind watched amused as a red-faced barrow boy, smelling of beer, thrust his face within a few inches of Wendy's to tell her in a hoarse whisper about his small son's skin complaint, as if Wendy didn't know.

'Still bad, is it, you'll have to take him to Outpatients again.'

'He won't go . . . says he'll only go into your ward. Could the wife bring him up, just so you could have a dekko?'

'All right, but it will have to be on an Outpatients' day and he'll have to see at least one doctor.'

The man took his chicken and chips, winked and left. 'Nice friends you have,' said Rosalind.

'That's all I needed. They feed that child on all the wrong food. He's had every test going for allergies and they know what foods to avoid, but he comes back every three months or so to be sorted out. I think he likes it with us. He's a bright boy and we give him more books to read in one week than he sees in a year at home.'

The fish looked delicious and they were very hungry. Clutching their moist parcels, they walked back along the road, in the shadow of the high buildings. 'Not the most dignified way of buying a meal, but who cares? I can hardly wait,' said Rosalind.

'I *can't* wait,' said Wendy, tearing away a corner of the paper and inserting a couple of fingers. She found a long potato chip and nibbled. 'Um . . . wonderful and piping hot. Try one.'

'Not until we get inside.' The smell released from the wrapping was growing and seemed to surround them as Wendy foraged for another chip. They reached the entrance and looked about them, giggling nervously. While the purchase of such food was no crime, they both knew that it wasn't quite the thing for sisters to be seen eating out of paper parcels late at night, outside the hospital.

'Come on, hurry across, there's nobody about.' Wendy clutched her package and ran to the Nurses' Home.

Rosalind followed, more slowly and gasped as a shadow loomed up before her, blocking her path as a car door slammed and from behind a jutting low wall, strode a man, intent on going into the same place as Wendy had reached. He brushed against the girl who stood with her fish and chip parcel in her hands. The white paper package fell to the ground and for the second time that day, two heads crashed together as Mr Peregrine Bradford bent to help the girl with honey blonde hair pick up the still intact but fishily fragrant pack. He held it out, a mocking smile on his lips. Rosalind shook her hair over her face, mumbled thanks and fled for the entrance, gaining it seconds before he appeared. She looked back, once, as if all the devils in hell were after her and ran into the kitchen where Wendy was convulsed with laughter.

'What's he doing back here? Is there another emergency? Should I ring Casualty?'

'Calm down. He has a room here and uses it when he has early cases or if he's worried about a patient.' She put the fish in the oven to make sure that it was really hot and they made coffee and found cutlery. The good food and coffee soothed Rosalind and when they washed the plates and tidied the sink, she was able to laugh about her encounter.

In a way, it put him into perspective as a man like ordinary men, didn't it? He was just another man . . . She left Wendy poring over a magazine that someone had left in the sitting room and went slowly towards the stairs. Bed would be nice, with so much to face tomorrow. Her one blessing was that he had not recognised her. She turned the key in her lock and sensed rather than saw a figure at the end of the corridor. Her long hair fell over her eyes as she tried to unlock her door with the wrong key and she didn't see him pause before climbing the next flight of stairs.

For a moment, he stared, his eyes without expression. She tossed back her hair and the key fitted. He saw the lovely face with the widely-spaced green eyes and the clear childlike skin and his expression changed as if he indeed was looking at a lovely, funny child.

CHAPTER FOUR

'CAN'T stay,' said Sister Rosalind Mason, drinking the last of her coffee.

'But you've hardly eaten a thing and it's early yet.'

'I've already been hard at it for an hour. I could kill that man, Wendy. I've been here for one day and he thrusts this lot at me.'

'Don't worry. I'm sure it will go well and Nurse Stephen is very good. You have done this kind of work before and even if Mr Bradford's technique is different, the human body remains the same.'

Rosalind relaxed. 'I'm glad I saw you. I shall try to remember what you said when everything is going wrong! I remember someone telling me the best way to go for an interview—it was to imagine the solemn examiner wearing long underpants.' Wendy snorted with laughter. 'It wouldn't work here . . . most of the time we *see* them wearing something similar.' She sighed. 'Where is the glamour of the theatre that everyone talks about?' But her face was relaxed and her lips twitched with delicious humour.

'Does poor old Mr Bradford wear jockey-longs?'

'I've no idea, and he isn't all that old, is he? For a consultant, I mean,' she added, hastily. 'Have you heard how Belinda is this morning?' she said to change the subject. 'I saw the night sister and she was very pleased with her. She sat up and demanded ice cream at four this morning.'

'It never fails. When they come in for tonsils we promise them ice cream as soon as they can take it. Actually, it does a lot of good and it slips down easily with little effort, the cold acting as a local anaesthetic and contracting the blood vessels.'

Rosalind walked rapidly to the theatre, casting one last look at the bright morning. The last I shall see of you today, she thought. Over the roof tops, the sun was lazily gold and the shimmering leaves trembled in a light breeze. The air was pure and a walk in the neighbouring park would have been better than being incarcerated in a darkened operating theatre for hours and hours. The theatre lights were all on, leaving not a corner without illumination. No dust, no dirt would dare to lurk there under the careful watch of the theatre staff. The tiled walls gleamed clean and the faint smell of antiseptics and anaesthetics came through the wide double doorway as the first patient was wheeled into the annexe to be induced before going into the theatre.

Few patients saw the inside of the beautiful modern theatre, as they were asleep before the main doors opened to admit them. Alan King was ready, his mask tied tightly for a change, and his light brown eyes laughing. 'What kept you?' he said, as Rosalind peeped in before going to her office to change.

'I've done a day's work already,' she said, and escaped, conscious that this was the first time he had seen her without a shapeless gown covering her from head to boots. He had the most disconcerting eyes that took in every detail of her face and body, his gaze lingering on the swelling curves under the well-fitting bodice. She changed quickly and went into the theatre. The door to the surgeon's room was shut. A smile lit up her green eyes, made even more brightly green by the green mask she had put on to show that she was the sister of the department even though she wasn't scrubbing and putting on theatre green. The dirty nurses and onlookers wore white and the small group of yawning students who gathered in the observation gallery needed to wear nothing in the way of protective clothing as they were sealed away beyond the glass screen.

Someone tested the inter-com between the theatre and gallery and one of the students groaned and remarked audibly that they'd have to be quiet as Bradford would hear and ask questions, mostly unanswerable. The audio-visual unit was turned on so that the operations could be relayed and the microscope was ready to fix to the table once the patient was in position. The junior nurse wrote the name, age and condition of the first case on the board and students took notes.

The door to the surgeon's room opened and Mr Peregrine Bradford stood there, wearing theatre boots, cap and mask and theatre pyjama trousers, but he was naked from the waist up. Rosalind stared and was glad that her expression was hidden by the mask she wore. 'Looks like a pirate, doesn't he?' chuckled Nurse Stephen as she held her gloved hands high before her and made a careful way to the first of the covered sterile trolleys.

A pirate, a beautiful, virile, tight-muscled pirate with a pair of deeply blue eyes that held more than a hint of steel. A fine haze of dark hair covered his chest, the line continuing down to the waist and disappearing below the belt of the loose trousers. He glanced round the room and nodded briefly to Nurse Stephen, before striding to the scrubbing bay to prepare. Rosalind watched as the jet of water from the foot-operated taps splashed the sink edge and sent a fine spray over the crisp hairs, making his chest look as if a powdering of fairy diamonds had fallen on him. She wanted to take a towel and dry them, slowly and carefully, and her cheeks burned as the eroticism of the imagined act came to her consciousness. She turned away, glad that it wasn't her job to wait on him at that moment.

The patient was in position, padded and supported comfortably in case this was to be a long session, his head turned away from the surgeon, with the affected ear uppermost. Quickly, the shaved area behind the ear was swabbed with antiseptic spirit-based dye and the sterile towels swathed in such a fashion that the operation area was exposed, but the rest of the patient was covered with towels on which instruments and swabs could be laid without making them unsterile. The surgeon stood waiting, hands high in front of him, in his green gown. Rosalind fixed the microscope casing into the slots on the special attachment to the table and slipped the microscope into it, making sure the line up with the painted area was true. More sterile towels were put round the parts of the instrument that might touch a scrubbed assistant or

the surgeon and only the eye pieces were left bare.
The adjustments could be controlled through the
sterile towel and so the surgeon was independent of
other help and could adjust as he wanted it.

'Right . . . all right with you, Alan?'

Dr Alan King nodded. The intra-laryngeal tube
was in position, with the gases from the anaesthetic
machine flowing at a strictly regulated rate through
it to the lungs, while making no impediment to the
surgeon. The monitors flickered and recorded the
condition of the man on the table and Mr Bradford
glanced up at the gallery. The house surgeon who
had felt faint the day before was shuffling uneasily
from foot to foot, and Rosalind saw that he was
wearing gloves far too big for him. She wondered
how he would get on when the first incision was
made and if he could bear the sound of bone
crunching. It was strange that most people could
watch very bloody operations when towels and
swabs were slung on the floor and the theatre
looked more like an abattoir than a place of healing, but few could stay in an ear, nose and throat
theatre without some undercurrent of unease.

The trolley of fine instruments was uncovered
and the operation began. The house surgeon wasn't
needed for the first part and stood with hands held
high as he had been told, but he stood too close to
the surgeon and had to step back hurriedly as he
turned to the trolley to see what was there. He
touched the gown of a nurse and, at once, at least
two voices said, 'Gloves.'

Mr Bradford muttered about the liability of in-
competent house surgeons and told him to change

his gloves. Rosalind went with the crestfallen young man and watched him strip off the contaminated gloves and throw them into the bin. 'Just as well you did that,' she said, cheerfully.

'How come?'

'Those are much to big. You'd never get your fingers into tiny holes if you had half an inch of free rubber flapping at the ends of your fingers. Here, take these, ease them on carefully and flex your fingers well when they are on.' The fresh pair fitted like the proverbial glove! and he smiled. 'Better?' she said. 'Stay for a minute, he's busy.' He looked at her enquiringly. 'He's making the first grab and I don't think you'd like it.' He paled over his mask. 'Now remember,' she whispered, 'avoid watching the first incision until you are sure you can take it. You'll be fine now,' she said, with a bracing smile. 'Go in and don't waste any more gloves.'

The lights were off except for the one over the drug trolley which was screened from the table. The surgeon's headlight and the light in the microscope were the only visible spots of brightness, but Alan King inspected his cylinders and trolley by means of a muted light attached to the side away from the table. From time to time, he watched the slim form in the shapeless gown, flitting about the theatre like a silent dryad, ensuring order and making the smooth running of the department perfect. The admiration in his eyes was partly for her gentle control of her job and partly for her grace and the attraction he had felt when first he saw the shapely lips twitching in a mischievous smile.

The stirrup-shaped and tiny bone called the

stapes in the middle ear was exposed and showed that it was no longer able to move and so transmit sound through the middle ear by means of vibrations. Increasing deafness had made the operation necessary as the bone hardened and became more dense. Once the small window, the fenestration, was done and the stapes carefully removed, Mr Bradford took the replacement, a tiny false stapes less than 5 millimetres in length, which was inserted and secured. Seen through the microscope, it looked large and manageable, but seen with the naked eye it showed just how delicate this work had become.

'What are his chances of restored hearing?' the surgeon asked the gallery when the main tension of the procedure was over and he could relax a little.

Some said very little could be expected, some said the prognosis was fairly good.

'I hope that your opinion of my surgery falls short of the reality,' he said, caustically. 'This man came in once and had the stapes forcibly rendered more mobile and his hearing was improved for a while, but the oto-sclerosis increased with further deposits of bone and we were back to the beginning. We now have a restored stapes, even if it is an artificial one, and if he doesn't have completely normal hearing in that ear, I shall be very surprised. In ninety per cent of all cases this is so with this technique.'

A ripple of approval came from the gallery, and Rosalind saw the proud stiffness of the man's back resolve into flexion as he bent over to examine the final result before leaving the dressing to Nurse

Stephen. Coffee was ready in the surgeon's room and the students in the gallery pushed their way out quickly, to be back for the second case in fifteen minutes. The next case was laid for and the theatre cleared quickly as there was little blood in that type of operation if all went well. She drank coffee and looked out at the morning through the balcony window.

She glanced towards the door. Once more she had worn the disc on a silver chain round her neck, forgetting to take it off from the night before when she went out with Wendy. It was uncomfortable as she had to bend down, stretch and generally change her position many times during a list and the chain became entangled in the metal catch of her bra strap. She fished for the chain and drew it up, found the clasp and put the chain and pendant on the edge of the table. She started as someone tapped on the door. 'Come in,' she said.

'Just checking on Belinda Sykes—I like to see them at least once and I haven't time for a full round today. Five minutes, Sister?'

'Yes, Mr Bradford . . . but you can't wear those.' He still wore the gown in which he had operated. That was permitted as it would be discarded before he scrubbed for the next case, but theatre boots were only worn in the theatre and not even a top surgeon could be allowed to forget it. 'Nurse! Fetch Mr Bradford's shoes. He can change in here.' He regarded her soberly and obediently slipped his feet from the boots. The nurse came with his highly polished handmade leather shoes and he put them on, leaving his boots by the desk.

'May I use that door? I can come in from the corridor and put my boots on again in here,' he said, politely. She nodded, relieved to see that he accepted the rule and wasn't angry. He left quickly. But why should I be relieved? she thought. He knows the rules and he'd have no right to be angry with me or anyone else who told him to change. She checked the trolley for the next batch of instruments and made sure that the drum of dressings contained enough for the next case. As she went back to the office to look at the book in which every operation was recorded and signed by the person in charge, she saw the surgeon return and bend to change his boots again. Hurriedly, she turned back to the sterilising room and alerted the team, and heard the sound of the lift doors as the next patient arrived.

She hesitated. He was taking his time in there, and she wanted to make notes about the last case before other matters crowded in and might make her forget just what had been done. She glanced through the frosted glass. He had gone. The shoes lay neatly together by the desk and she called the junior to take them to the surgeons' room. 'They have their own room,' she said. 'We don't want them taking over everything.'

The next case went smoothly and by the time the mastoid was ready, the atmosphere was light and conversation had started, always a good sign that the surgeon was pleased with his own efforts.

'This isn't a bad one,' said Mr Bradford. 'I think it needs draining, but we don't have to do anything very heroic. There's a good chance that we can leave the middle ear and just do a cortical excision of the mastoid process.'

Some of the students left and the microscope was already packed away safely in its case. The lights were on dimly and everyone seemed to walk more freely and speak in normal voices. To her surprise, Rosalind was enjoying herself and full of reluctant admiration for the way that the man did his work. Arrogant he might be, rude he certainly was when an instrument was dropped or a swab not ready when he put out an imperious hand for it, expecting the right thing to be put in his hand without him asking for it, but most surgeons were like that in moments of stress, and he instructed the students, worked steadily and fast while giving the impression that he was taking his time, left nothing to chance and invited comment from the others in the theatre.

Alan King sat behind his machines with a bored expression on his face. He had nothing to do now that the patient was induced and there would be little change in the drugs and gases given while the operation was in progress. Rosalind decided that he was very good at his particular job and that he hid a fertile brain under his air of casual tolerance. He watched her as she went about her work and tried to make her look at him, but she contrived to stay on the other side of the room as much as possible.

'Ring down to the ward,' she said to a junior nurse. 'They can send a nurse with the trolley now.' She told the junior nurse to make sure that all the swabs were collected at once and put into the bin for the incinerator. Nurse Stephen was applying a very dashing mastoid bandage to the semi-conscious patient and Alan King turned off the cylinders, threw the used intra-trachial tube into a dish on the bottom shelf of his trolley, stretched and yawned.

Rosalind was conscious of someone behind her as she talked to the junior nurse. 'Why must these swabs be carefully burned, Nurse?' said Peregrine Bradford. 'Sister is right, of course, but why those more than the others from the first two cases?' He still wore his mask and it was impossible to know if he was teasing or deadly serious.

'I was going to ask,' said the junior, nervously.

'Infection—remember that this theatre deals with two kinds of cases. We do the clean ones at the beginning of the list and the dirty ones last. If those grossly infected dressings were left, and contaminated anything used for a clean operation, we might, probably would, have trouble.' He swung round to the house surgeon who was hovering near. 'What trouble could be introduced, even by airborne organisms?'

'Sepsis, sir.'

'I know that, even the most junior nurse knows that.'

'Er . . . abscess?'

'Yes, we could even have that as a complication here, but I think we've cured him. The spectre that should haunt every self-respecting surgeon is meningitis, introduced surgically, or by absorption through the mucous membrane of the ear, nose or throat.' He tore at his mask and threw it to the floor. His eyes were gentian blue, and haunted. He removed his gown and the sweat was damp on his shoulders after the exertion and concentration of the morning. He seemed to have forgotten his audience and stared at the young woman who was watching him anxiously, her green eyes clouded, her lips trembling, watching him, listening to him and wondering why he was so intense about something that was in every text book and happened at some time in many scrupulously clean theatres. Had he experienced such a case and did he hold himself responsible?

He gave a short laugh. 'Never forget it. Never let up on after-care, Doctor, and keep a sharp look out for adverse symptoms post-operatively.' He was back to normal, asking wickedly unanswerable questions with a fiendish smile of triumph when his house surgeon blushed and faltered over the replies. Rosalind raised her eyebrows and found Alan King smiling at her, catching her off guard.

'He's very pleased with himself. I think I'll get out before he gets too insufferable.' He walked with Rosalind to her office. 'Did you make a note of the first case? Did I give a full dose of thio-pentone ... I like to keep check?' It was an innocent request and she went into the office. He followed, closing the door after him. 'Alone at last,' he said, lazily. 'At last . . . and I can get a really good look at you. Aren't you going to take off that awful gown and cap and let me catch a glimpse of that tantalising hair, which I suspect must come well beyond your shoulders.'

'I shall change when I've checked the theatre,'

she said, abruptly. 'Now, the book is there and I
have work to do.' He stood between her and the
door. 'Please Dr King . . .'

'Call me Alan and I'll let you go. Everyone does,
and it's a mite more friendly, for someone who is
going to be a friend, a very close friend?'

She tried to evade him by side-stepping to the
door, then made for the other door leading to the
corridor. She stopped, looking down at her own
theatre boots. She couldn't set a bad example after
telling the surgeon that he couldn't use that way out
wearing theatre boots. Alan King was grinning.
'Please let me through, Alan.'

'That's better, and very prettily it falls from your
lovely lips . . . such lovely lips.'

She stepped cautiously towards the door and he
stood aside. She was level with him when he
reached across and seized her, spinning her to face
him and putting her off balance. His mouth
brushed her cheek as she tried to struggle free. He
gripped her more tightly and she stepped back,
seeing a figure appear through the shadowed glass.
'Don't be a fool, Alan, don't be a fool.'

The door opened behind the surprised man and a
voice that once more held the cold sharpness of
crisply broken ice came through the half open door.
'I think I left my shoes here. I'm *so* sorry to disturb
you, Sister. I realise that in your position you have
certain privileges in your own private office, but
although this glass is fairly efficient, it isn't completely opaque.'

'I sent your shoes back to the surgeons' room, Mr
Bradford, they are under the table.' She pushed her

crooked cap back from her face, and tendrils of gold escaped to curl round her frightened eyes. Alan King smirked and made for the corridor entrance. 'I'm sorry,' said Rosalind in a small voice. 'He, that is . . .' The tears welled up making great pools of emerald. Her lips were full and quivering and the man gazed down at her, a tiny nerve twitching under one eye.

'Oh, come now, Sister. It isn't the end of the world when a man like that makes a pass.' The voice held no warmth, no understanding. The harsh syllables carved deep wounds into her heart. 'But if you wanted to repulse him, calling him by his first name on such slight acquaintance isn't exactly the best way to do so. If he attracts you so strongly that you allow such liberties—which is your business, not mine—may I suggest some time off duty? I'm sure he will suggest it very soon.' His mouth was hard with anger and something more. The beautiful hands were tense, his blue silk shirt sent stabs of azure into his now grey-blue eyes and he struggled to say or, perhaps, not to say something more. The green pools brimmed and overflowed, sending tiny rivers of tears down her cheeks, silently.

'Stop it!' The voice was even more harsh. 'Do you expect me to kiss away those tears, now that he has gone? Are you such a child? If he means nothing, laugh it off . . . it's no use expecting an old man like me to understand.'

He padded away in stockinged feet back to the surgeons' room and shut the door behind him. Rosalind dabbed her eyes. She took off her gown and tidied her hair, quickly applied cleansing cream and fresh makeup and went back to the theatre. The theatre was nearly clean and Nurse Stephen had gone to lunch with the junior and the runner. It was good to be alone, giving herself time to recover. 'Men!' she said. She called Alan King all the names she could think of and then dared to think of the other man who had stood in the doorway . . . She giggled, rather hysterically—like a Peregrine in stockinged feet. The proud, angry head, the taut neck and the slightly ruffled feathers over the temples.

She tried to be angry at his tone and the anger badly suppressed that had threatened to erupt as the blue eyes darkened and hardened. He hadn't touched her . . . the only physical contact they had made was when their two heads had clashed, but she had felt his nearness across an intangible band of silk that wanted to draw them closer together. She carefully returned the instruments to their cases and smiled. The fact that he had mentioned her tears, and the possibility of kissing them away, must mean that he had thought of doing so, if only in his sub-conscious mind.

'How old is Mr Bradford?' she asked Nurse Stephen when she came back from lunch.

'I don't know, just the right age, I'd say.'

'For what?'

'Please yourself . . .' she shrugged and grinned. 'I think he's marvellous, but he'll never see me further than on the end of a needle holder.

'He said he was an old man,' said Rosalind, casually.

Her staff nurse gave her a searching glance. 'In my experience, men say that when they've been accused of baby-snatching.'

'Oh, is he going out with a young nurse?'

'The day anyone knows anything about him will be the end of the world. Maybe he is, maybe he has a wife stuck away in the country . . . I think we've run out of maybes as far as he is concerned.'

Rosalind went back to the office to fetch her cloak before going to lunch and suddenly missed her chain and disc. She picked up books from the desk and looked underneath. She shifted papers and opened the desk drawers. The floor gave no clue and she turned out the waste paper basket, but the disc had gone. I know I had it in here, she thought. She thought back to the time when Alan King had followed her into the office. That was the answer. It was just the sort of thing he would do and then try to tease her with it. He might even dangle it before her, trying to extract a date from her as a condition of her having it back again. It wasn't worth a great deal . . . but it was galling to lose anything that had become as familiar to her as that pendant. She bit her lip. The meaning of the symbols would be plain to him, too, the male and female entwined . . . the emblem of sex and life.

The dark-haired attractive sister from Orthopaedics was at second lunch and although they had met very briefly, they sat together, bound by similar jobs and interests. 'Settling in?' said Anna Forsythe, with a smile.

'In at the deep end today,' said Rosalind. They discussed the new theatre complex and naturally the discussion included the surgeons. 'I enjoyed the list with Mr Murray,' said Rosalind.

'And what about Perry?'

'Mr Bradford?' Rosalind nearly choked over her fish. How could anyone call that man Perry in such a familiar way?

'He's a bit dour at times, but a heart of gold. We're very fond of him and Slade had rooms with him at one time when they were students together.'

A faint smile hovered at the corners of her mouth as Rosalind said, 'I can't imagine him as a student. He's much too elegant and smooth . . . in his dress, that is.'

'And a little abrasive in his manner?' She got up to get coffee and brought two cups. 'He's shy and takes life a little too seriously at times, but he's great fun. You'll grow to love him.' Anna was laughing. 'I shall have to give him a lecture. He promised me that he'd be nice to the new sister.'

'Why was that necessary? Did he scare away the last one?'

Anna glanced at the set expression of the girl at her side and noticed the vulnerability of her mouth. 'No, he didn't scare her and he shouldn't scare you, either. It was just a joke.' She smiled. 'We teased him because one of the nurses had a crush on him some time ago and he was rather rude to her.'

'Well, at least I shan't offend in that way,' said Rosalind with more vehemence than she intended. 'He's already as good as told me I'm childish and insufferable and I readily return his feelings. I shall continue to enjoy my sessions with Mr Murray and put up with Sir when I have to do so.' She saw the disapproving glance. 'Well, even you as his friend must admit that it's too bad to have three major cases in one morning beginning at eight-thirty? It might have worked in the days when staff lived on the premises, but my senior staff nurse lives out and so does the junior. They live in the hostel, it's true, but that's not like walking from one block to the next ready for duty.'

'Do you know why he started early?'

'You might know, but I don't. He didn't see fit to make any excuse, just laughed and went off as if well-satisfied that he'd got his own way.'

'He wouldn't say, I know that, but not for the reason you think . . . he wasn't going off for a half day's golf or something like that.'

'What then?' asked Rosalind reluctantly.

'He has a clinic for deaf children that he has started in the cottage hospital near Reading. The place was closing but he fought to retain it as a building to house clinics. They let him have it on condition he found a good use for it that needed no trained staff or bed occupancy.' She paused. 'The energy of the man. He got together some of the brightest young doctors and surgeons and they hold clinics payed for by voluntary sources—charities with an interest in each faculty. Perry has a retired speech therapist who helps in his clinic, there are educational sessions for parents with children suffering from allergic conditions like urticaria and those needing details of special diets,' she paused.

'All this can be done in such centres and the results are good. They even have a local club for parents with Downs Syndrome babies who can meet and know that they aren't the only families affected.'

'I didn't know,' said Rosalind. 'But I can't think why he had to go there dressed up as if he was visiting royalty. Surely that must hit the wrong note if mothers think he's just another rich consultant more interested in clothes, cars and status than in people?'

Anna smiled. 'He dressed like that because he had private patients on his visiting list here and you weren't far out when you said visiting royalty. He has to have lunch with a very important and rich man who is on the verge of giving a lot of money to this project and he couldn't exactly go to Claridges in casual clothes could he?'

'Oh, Anna, I feel ashamed . . .' She smiled. 'But it doesn't explain everything. I still feel much more comfortable with Mr Murray than with him.'

'Well, you won't be worried by him for a week. He's on leave as from tomorrow. I hope you're not off this weekend. What a waste to be off at the same time as someone you dislike.' She laughed and looked at her watch. 'Now, I *am* off and I'm winkling out my darling husband before he decides to stay here for the weekend. We have a place in the country with no telephone! It's bliss.'

Rosalind watched her go and envied her. She was in love, she had a job she liked and she was near to her husband. 'If only . . .' she murmured. What was she saying? Only yesterday she wanted nothing more than a good career and a happy atmosphere in which to work and now she was wondering what it was like to love, really to love and be loved by the one man who could make her happy. The man in her mind was faceless, but she could close her eyes and feel his hidden strength. She walked back to the theatre, trying to tear her concentration back to sterilisers and away from a woman's face that spoke of love, a woman who sincerely liked Peregrine Bradford. Perry, the man who she could hate . . . admire . . . but never ignore.

She saw Alan King going towards his car, keys in hand and she dodged back so that he wouldn't see her. I shall never mention the pendant, she vowed. If he asks, I'll deny all knowledge of it and his joke will fall flat. She was fortunate in the fact that none of the nurses knew she had the pendant. The only person who had seen it was Wendy, and she had shown little interest.

'Now, off you go and have a wonderful day off,' she said to her delighted staff nurse. 'Thanks to you, I know I can now cope with anything that comes.' Brave words, knowing that it would be only Tony Murray with whom she would have to work if a case came in.

CHAPTER FIVE

'SISTER Mason?'

'Yes . . . who is that?'

'Claud from the lodge, Sister. There's a car for you. He said he'd wait.' The line went dead and when she tried to get him back, Claud didn't answer.

Rosalind ran back up the stairs and caught up her handbag and umbrella. Flecks of rain against her window early that morning had made her decide that even if she didn't abandon her idea of exploring a street market on her Sunday morning off, she must take an umbrella and wear something warm. She had ordered no taxi and the thought of all that money ticking away on the clock appalled her. It must be for some other person who was patiently waiting for a call from the porter.

She buttoned up the crimson knitted coat that had been her last real extravagance and thrust a head scarf into the pocket. She had coiled her hair up into a macaroon at the back of her head and knew that it would remain fairly neat through the day, even with the wind rising as it seemed to be now.

She reached the lodge and tapped on the shutter, but there was no reply. 'Damn,' she said, and looked for the taxi, but there was only one car waiting by the gate. A figure in a short raincoat walked towards her, smiling. 'Have you seen Claud?' asked Rosalind.

'Of course. I got him to ring you.' The calm voice was infuriating as Alan King put a hand under her elbow to lead her to the car. She drew away. 'Don't be like that,' he said, with a little-boy-lost-look that had worked wonders with so many nurses. 'I knew you had a day off and were all alone in the big city, so what else could I do?'

'Do you want me to tell you?' said Rosalind, shortly.

'Ah, come on, be nice. I am all alone too. What could be nicer than a drive out to a very good little pub I know, a bite to eat and a long walk if the weather holds?'

'Nothing could be nicer with someone I like, but after your behaviour in the theatre, I wouldn't touch you with a ten-foot pole!' She shook his hand from her arm.

'You were going out. I deduce that from that very sexy coat you're wearing and the umbrella seems to say you are going further than the local church. Buses are terrible on Sunday mornings and there is no tube station near.' He smiled, triumphantly.

'I have an appointment,' she said, with a sweet smile. 'I have an appointment with someone expecting me in Town.' She enjoyed his change of expression. 'I *do* have friends in London,' she added, 'and this afternoon I have a date to play tennis here, so I have to get back early.'

'Let me give you a lift. I promise to behave like a

little gentleman and not to lay a finger on you, even if the urge is overwhelming.'

She hesitated and saw the bus sweep past the end of the road. There wouldn't be another to take her right into London for another half an hour. 'You've made me miss my bus,' she said. He stood by the car and she remembered what Wendy had said of him, that he would be all right once he got the message that there was to be no nonsense. In fact, she knew that if he behaved she would welcome him as a friend. His humour and undoubted efficiency in the theatre had impressed her even when she was furious with him. 'Look,' she said, gently. 'We are going to have to work together and so far, I have been very happy to do so—as far as work is concerned, but if you make one more pass at me, I shall hit you with my umbrella!' She laughed as she spoke, but there was no misreading the resolution in the green eyes.

'OK. I give in. I'll drive you to Town, drop you off and hope to see you this evening at the music club . . . how's that?'

'Fine, and I am grateful for the lift.' But she wondered what he would have said if she confessed that she was going to a street market . . . alone.

'Where are you meeting your friend?'

She did a hasty re-think of her morning. 'Er . . . I'm going to Charing Cross Station,' she said, knowing that he couldn't drive in and see her meet her fictitious friend and he would find it impossible to park and accompany her. 'If you could drop me off by the station, I can be there in time.' She made it sound as if she was late so that he wouldn't ask her to go for coffee or a drink first. He sighed, settled her into the passenger seat and drove away, through the windswept streets, along the main road over the river at Vauxhall and along the Embankment.

'Some day, if you find you can trust me, I'd like to take you on the river,' he said.

'I'd like that,' she said, and smiled. He was rather sweet when he wasn't trying to be Casanova. So far, he hadn't trotted out the old 'my wife doesn't understand me', routine and she took it to be a compliment to her intelligence. I wonder if he *is* married? He's here on Sunday morning with time on his hands. If he was married, he'd be home for as many weekends as his duties permitted. She glanced at the good-looking profile and decided that he was more unhappy than he admitted. 'Thanks a lot,' she said, as the car slid to an impressive stop right by the station, on double yellow lines. 'I'll get out quickly or you might have a ticket.' She smiled back through the window and half wished that she'd asked him to come with her.

'Until this evening,' he said, and drove away, without another glance at her. She walked to the underground station and took the tube to Bow, studying her London A-Z as she was hurled between the stations. The street market in Roman Road of which she had heard must be quite close to the tube. As usual, it was further than she'd imagined, but she was enjoying the brisk walk after the confines of the theatre. A whole day off, after a very pleasant week when she had coped with nearly every type of Ear, Nose and Throat procedure with

Mr Tony Murray operating and the house surgeon showing real promise when he attempted his first, well-supervised tonsil list and antra washouts.

Ahead, she saw the clutter of market stalls stretching away along the road that was blocked off for the market. It was easy to see all the stalls as they had to follow the line of the road, there being no central square as there were in many small town markets. I can go along one side and back the other, she thought, with satisfaction, then I shan't miss anything. It was fascinating to listen to the quick-witted banter of the men selling everything from bath towels to mouse traps, from candy to antiques and everything in between. The cheeky and often suggestive patter was amusing here and the crowds, gathered to look for bargains—a morning's entertainment, were tolerant and good humoured. She watched a demonstration of a food slicer and was offered a sample of jellied eels which she refused. She bought tights and a sweater of misty purple that was a real bargain, walked on and found the stalls loaded with antiques, junk and novelties. She held a long string of beads in her hand, then put them down again. There were chains and bracelets and more chains . . . slender this time with pendants and discs, mock jewels in bright colours and little plaques bearing slogans, most of which were too obscene to wear. She drifted on to a similar stall where the merchandise was more restrained and artistic. Here there were other discs. She stopped.

A group of Americans, smartly-suited and smoothly coiffured were examining the wares and the stall holder was doing his best to sell. 'Genuine copies of Greek gods you got there. Just the thing to take home . . . a bit of culture. We got Homer and Venus . . . and lots of old geezers with fuzz . . . philosophers an' all. That's Chinese . . . good luck charms . . . Cornish pixies . . . you name it, we've got it.'

Rosalind paused, amused, and looked up at the rack on which hung dozens of charms. Her hand touched a disc of silver and black and she saw that it was like the one she had lost. It might not be of such good quality, the other being of genuine silver and she had her doubts about the truth of the description given so generously by the man selling them, but they were almost the same and she realised how much she had missed her lost charm on its slender chain.

Strange that Alan King had made no reference to it, when she was sure that it was he who had taken it from the desk top in her office the day that Mr Peregrine Bradford had operated all the morning and found Alan King trying to kiss her. Her cheeks still burned each time she thought of it. The fact that Peregrine Bradford had been away for a whole week had given her a breathing space in which to gain experience of the theatre and confidence in her own abilities once more. She was in control of her staff, and the work she had to do, and had built up a warm rapport with the other doctors and surgeons who used the ENT unit. The loss of her talisman and the embarrassing events of that morning were irrevocably linked in her memory.

I shall never ask Alan King for the charm, I shall

pretend to everyone that I lost it when I was out in the street, she told herself. After all, chains break at unexpected moments. But the chains swung gently and silver and black rotated as the Yin and Yang turned. I must have one, she thought. She smiled to herself. It would be fun to get one and if Alan produced it as a trophy he had taken from her, she could show him the new one with an air of complete innocence as if the one he had was not hers. The man behind the stall saw her smile. 'Want one, Luv? Just the thing for a pretty girl . . . very sexy.' The Americans smiled and one woman bought two, for the nieces back home. Rosalind selected one and it was wrapped in a screw of pink tissue paper torn from a box lining. She dropped it into her bag and looked for blue and white china that she wanted for her aunt's birthday.

It must be good to have a place of one's own where a collection could be made over the years, she thought. She lingered over two small dishes, wishing she could afford both. I've changed, I'm growing up and wanting my own flat where I can keep my own accumulation of junk and have somewhere to call my own, she thought. The pretty room in the Nurses' Home would be hers for as long as she was on the staff of the Princess Beatrice Hospital, with complete freedom to use as she wished, and she could leave her belongings there even if she went away for a long holiday, a privilege not given to nurses in training who lived in the hospital buildings. It should be enough, but during the time she had been at Beattie's, the urge to spread herself had come.

It's not as if I had a boy friend and wanted to settle down and make a nest. I can't imagine marrying any of the boys I've met, either here or in the other training school. She thought back to the students who had pursued her, making no secret of the fact that they were interested in sex rather than a permanent loving partnership, although she had felt that one or two only needed the right encouragement and she would by now be married. They were fun, but that was all. She left the market and hurried back to the tube station. It was early enough to go back to lunch and get changed for tennis. The rain had come to nothing and patches of blue appeared between the high clouds. It would be great to beat hell out of a few tennis balls.

The tube train rumbled through the dark, giving off the smell that could be generated only in those dim tunnels. She went out to find the bus that would take her within a hundred yards of the hospital, and examined her pendant while she waited for the bus to come. It was as if she had found an old friend. It was just like the other one now that she had it away from the row of replicas and she rubbed the silver on her glove to make it shine. She put it carefully away when the bus arrived and almost hoped that Dr Alan King would show her the one he thought he had stolen from her. I'd love to see his face, she thought, wickedly.

A quick glance round the car park told her that Alan King had decided to stay away for lunch and she went to her room to leave her purchases. She was ten minutes early for lunch and sat on a low wall in the sun, enjoying the sudden burst of spring-like weather. The private-wing car park was emptying of morning visitors and only two large cars gleamed proudly in the sunshine. She watched them, idly, wondering to whom they belonged, and a sharp picture of another day came to her mind, of a man with dark hair, tinged with just enough grey to make him look mature and fascinating, who had stared at her for one moment as if he knew her.

He'll be back soon . . . and she wondered why her heart was heavy. What did it matter if he came or stayed away? She could now cope with everything the theatre threw at her and he was only another arrogant, bullying surgeon, the only one, in fact who was distasteful to her. And he'll have forgotten what he saw in my office . . . if it ever remained in his memory while he visited his friends.

'Are you going to sit there all afternoon?' Wendy was still in uniform and ready for lunch. 'I saw you from the corridor window and thought I was keeping you waiting, but no! Here she sits dreaming.' She laughed. 'Have a good morning? I tried to warn you but couldn't catch you.'

'Warn me?'

'You did go out with Alan King didn't you? He was asking about your off-duty last night and I had a feeling he might lay in wait for you.'

'He did, but I managed to stall him.'

'Good for you.'

'I accepted a lift up to Town, but pretended I had a date and was in a hurry. Don't give me away, will you.'

'He's quite fun and if you can manage him you'll

find him useful. At least he isn't all blushes and acne like the ENT house surgeon. Now I would find him *very* trying.'

'He's a pet.'

'He obviously thinks you're the best-looking woman around, and kind with it! Taken quite a shine to you, so be careful what you do with those great green eyes.'

'I only stopped him being sick, or passing out in theatre. He's still a bit wet behind the ears, but he's come on very well with Tony Murray this week.'

'I take it that you were glad to see the back of Peregrine?' They sat at an empty table in the dining room to eat the very well-served meal put before them. 'I like Sunday lunch here. It's like the old times when we had waitress service all the time.'

Sometimes, it was good to hear Wendy rabbiting on, not really expecting one answer in five to all her questions. Anna Forsythe joined them, dressed in well-cut cords and a huge but flattering pale yellow mohair sweater. Her cheeks glowed. 'Slade had to see a patient as soon as we got back so I thought I'd leave our main meal until this evening when he's free again.'

'You have a flat of your own?'

'Yes, we have a half-house up the hill with loads of room. Sometimes visiting doctors stay with us if they want to be near the hospital for a day or so, usually when we have a congress here or there is a paper being read in Town. The house is good for parties, too. You must come when we have another, but you know how it is, if I plan anything, either Slade or I have cases and we have to cancel it.

So, if I ring you and say come now, drop everything and come, quite informal and if you can bring cider or some food, that's nice too.'

Rosalind blushed with pleasure. 'I'd like that very much. Are you going to the music club tonight? Have you any idea what it is?'

'It's a Chopin evening, on tape mostly, but we have a Polish doctor here who plays very well and he comes and helps out,' said Wendy. 'I shall go, but the next one will be definitely out. *The Flying Dutchman* is too heavy-going for my poor old brain.'

Anna left as soon as she had eaten her first course. 'I have to unpack and get the food ready for tonight. I have so little time to cook that it's still a great pleasure, and when I *can* have dinner alone with my husband, it's bliss.'

'I thought you had him all to yourself this weekend? Quite a long weekend, wasn't it?' said Wendy.

'We had some time alone, but we had a guest staying with us. He enjoyed the fresh air and so did we, it was very good. The country cottage is fun but I feel that I'm putting down roots in that ugly house up the hill.'

'She's a very lucky woman,' said Wendy. 'She has everything a woman could want—interesting work and a husband who adores her, a lovely flat and plenty of friends.'

'She's very friendly,' said Rosalind, and hoped that she didn't sound lukewarm in her praise, but she knew she envied the radiant woman who had married a contemporary of the man who was in the back of her mind, refusing to be ignored even when he was miles away with his family. 'I suppose her husband is older than her,' she said.

'A few years, but don't you think that more experienced men have more to offer?'

'I wouldn't know,' said Rosalind. 'Are we going to play tennis, or have you eaten too much?'

A fine tilth of soil and fallen leaves showed that the hard courts hadn't been used much during the winter and the two hospital sisters spent the first ten minutes with enormous wide brooms clearing one of the courts. It was chilly with shorts and bare knees, but soon they were glowing and the sun shone all the afternoon. 'I should lose pounds,' panted Wendy. 'I haven't had as much exercise for months. I shall be a wreck in the morning.'

One or two nurses watched on their way to various parts of the hospital and Claud had to gawk at them in order to tell his friend from the psychiatric hospital lodge what the young sisters were getting up to. He was mildly surprised to see Sister Mason back so soon. After Dr King had slipped him a quid to ring the Nurses' Home and tell her a car was waiting, and then to push off and buy him a paper at the stand by the entrance, he didn't expect to see her playing tennis with Sister Fletcher. He grinned. She looked as if she could put Dr Bloody King in his place.

The game ended and Rosalind went round collecting tennis balls while Wendy loosened the net and hung it over the tape. One ball was through into an old part of the former garden. A patch was left that was neither patio nor garden and difficult to keep tidy as anyone trying to work there had to squeeze through a small gap.

She took a deep breath and eased her way through. 'Oh, NO!' she said as the wire caught in the front of her shirt, pulling at the thin material and threatening to tear it. 'Oh . . . I'm caught.' She tried to go back the way she'd come, but the rusty wire seemed to reach out thin talons to grip and tear, like a bird of prey, was her unbidden thought. She looked up, hoping to see Wendy, but she was talking to two nurses through the wire netting on the far side of the courts. 'Wendy!' she called. Windows overlooking the courts were like blind eyes that ignored her predicament. She tugged gently and felt the rip of cotton. This was serious. She unbuttoned her shirt, trying to see where the wire was catching. If I slide out of it, I can see it and the pressure will be off the material, she thought. She opened the front of the shirt and ducked down, leaving the garment on the wire. Another strand scratched her back and she carefully bent it away from her. Gradually, she bent back all the frayed wire, found the two pieces that had interlocked to make a trap for the fabric and painstakingly withdrew them.

She glanced anxiously at the windows but there was no movement there. She returned to her task, glad that the sun was warm and she was in a sheltered situation. Her soft bra barely covered her breasts, supporting rather than restraining, but comfortable for energetic games. A sound made her stare in horror at the ground floor window near to her. Curtains were across the windows indicating that the occupant was either away or sleeping, perhaps a house surgeon who had been up for half the previous night. The curtains were flung back and the window went up, almost in one movement. Another second and a pair of horrified green eyes stared into the slightly amused and completely baffled blue eyes of Peregrine Bradford, senior surgeon of the Ear, Nose and Throat department at the Princess Beatrice Hospital.

Rosalind crossed her hands over her bosom which only made the cleavage more pronounced. Her hair was escaping from the neat coil into which she had put it when she began the game, her breath came in jerky gasps and her face was flushed with exertion and embarrassment. She was also convinced that the shorts she had last worn on a beach were far too skimpy and revealing. I couldn't look worse if I was stark naked, she thought. She tried to wriggle back through the gap, clutching her torn shirt in her hand, but she forgot to turn sideways. Once more she was stuck.

The window was opened wider and Peregrine Bradford was there, taking her firmly by the arm and telling her to go limp. She obeyed, not because she wanted to do as he said, but because her knees no longer had the power to support her. She slid down and he eased her towards him. 'I want to go back,' she said.

'Impossible,' he said, calmly. He kept a firm hold on her, as if expecting her to escape and hurl herself at the wire. 'Come this way—you can get tidy and leave by a more conventional method, like a door.' His blue eyes were mocking. 'I don't know what the current rules are, although as a sister you have carte blanche, I believe, but is it now a habit to enter the rooms of medical staff through their windows?'

'I wasn't, I was looking for tennis balls.'

'You . . . were looking for tennis balls?' By this time they were standing on the carpet in a very pleasant masculine bedroom. He shut the window as if trapping a butterfly and laughed. His face was transformed, his eyes glittered and the well-formed lips parted to reveal perfect teeth. 'That beats everything. I've heard some excuses, but that's wonderful! I'll have to tell Matron to add that to her collection of excuses that nurses give when they are discovered in medical quarters.' He held the shirt in his hands and Rosalind could only hang her head in shame and humiliation. He thought she was an idiot and a child. She put out a hand for the shirt, and glanced up, pleading for escape.

'I'm getting cold,' she said. 'Thank you for letting me use your room, but I can manage now, Mr Bradford.' Her voice was as cool and prim as she could make it and it trembled only slightly.

'You can't go yet.' She looked startled. He was looking at her shoulder and moving towards her.

'Keep away,' she said.

'What's the matter? You can't go yet . . . your shoulder is covered with blood.' He swung her round so that she could look in the mirror and she saw the scratches bleeding on her back and shoulder.

'I'll have a bath when I get back . . . and the shirt's dirty now. I can wear it and take it off when I get back. It will save time.'

He was mocking again. 'Really Sister, with all your knowledge of hygiene! I can't let you do any such thing. What if there is soil or rust in that shirt . . . have you had an anti-tetanus injection lately?' He stopped smiling. 'Sit there and don't move! I shall be less than five minutes.' He gave her a paper tissue. 'Here . . . mop up with this if it shows signs of flooding my room.'

He was gone, shutting the door firmly behind him. Rosalind ventured to look about her at the deep green and gold curtains and the carpet that looked like bracken and heather and autumn leaves rolled into one warm muted colour. There were good hair brushes on the table and piles of books everywhere. On a stand was a music centre and a pile of discs and a case of tapes. Pictures of country scenes hung on the walls and a soft suitcase sat on the bed. The only sign of opulence was a wolf-skin rug, and a rather battered cagoule hung from a peg on the back of the door.

He came back with a bowl of warm water and put it on the table. He found a clean towel in a drawer and began to bathe the almost dry scratches. She tried to control the muscles in her back as his hands gently probed to find if there were pieces of wire in the skin. 'I'm sorry if I'm hurting you,' he said.

'It's all right,' she said . . . what did he know of the sensations that coursed down her spine? What could he know of the sensuous pain his slightest touch engendered? This was something she had never known, this feeling of lassitude . . . of yearning . . . of wonder.

'One thing about you I like.'

She came out of her pink haze. 'What?' and looked up at him with misted eyes.

'You have a fast clotting time.' He dried the last patch and dabbed all the scratches with something that smarted badly, then sprayed with a plastic wound cover. 'That should do.' He bent towards her and gently wiped a trickle of water from where her bra met her skin. 'I'll lend you something.' He rummaged in a drawer and produced a sweat shirt with the hospital rugby badge on it. 'More in keeping with your sportive image,' he said.

'Thank you.' She slipped it over her head and found that it was far too big for her. The sleeves hung over her hands and the shirt came down over her shorts, making her look as if she wore nothing but the all-enveloping garment. 'I can't wear this . . . I can put on the other one.'

'You'll do as I say, wear it and change into something almost as loose to give those scratches time to set.' He knelt before her and turned up the sleeves so that she could use her hands. He touched her hand and the same sensation coursed through her once more, as if a current of desire bound them together, but she could read nothing in the eyes hidden beneath the dark thick eyelashes, and he gave no hint of any answering feeling. He stood up and absentmindedly took a long strand of her fair hair and put it back behind her ear.

'I must look a mess,' she said, blushing.

'You do rather, but what did the poet say about a certain carelessness in the dress? She might have been like you.' He opened the door, abruptly, as if she had taken more than enough of his time. He stood back as she went, as if he wanted no further contact, and closed the door firmly as soon as she was in the corridor. She looked back at the closed door and was suddenly tired and very sad. Once more she had shown him what a fool she was and she couldn't have looked more dishevelled. It was only then that she remembered how he'd been dressed—in old clothes and muddy shoes, the cagoule still damp from a shower, his hair blown free giving him a reckless look of a man free of convention—so unlike the man in the smooth clothes and hand-made shoes.

CHAPTER SIX

'I STILL can't believe it,' said Wendy Fletcher. 'First I saw you looking for tennis balls and then you disappeared completely. I knew you hadn't passed me when I was talking to the nurses and there just *isn't* any other way out.'

Rosalind hoped that she would go and give her an opportunity to put the borrowed sweat shirt in a bag ready to return it to Peregrine Bradford at the earliest opportunity. She had hastily stuffed it under the bedcover when Wendy came to the door. A moment sooner and the sharp-eyed sister would have seen it spread on the bed and also seen the scratches on her back. She now wore a loose shirt with a gathered yoke and pretty embroidery which she tucked firmly into the waistband of a velvet skirt. 'I couldn't get back and my shirt was torn. Mr Bradford happened to look out of his window and asked me to go through his room back to the main block.'

'What's it like in his room? I bet you're the only woman here bar the cleaners to see in that holy of holies.' Her eyes sparkled. 'I hope the entire medical school saw you emerging from his room.'

'Don't be silly. I was there for only a few minutes.' She hadn't the courage to tell Wendy that she had sat in that room, practically naked, or so it seemed to her, while he tended her wounds and insisted on lending her his shirt.

'I'll go and put the kettle on now I've found you.' Wendy laughed. 'I know it's a magic day with the sun shining after all that terrible weather, must be magic for me to stir myself to play anything energetic,' she said and went down to the kitchen, singing.

Magic . . . you've no idea what magic was wrought by two gentle, masterful hands on a woman's back. Rosalind shivered as she recalled the frisson of sensuality that had almost overpowered her at his touch. To him it was nothing, such a tiny first-aid procedure for a first-class surgeon to have to do; the kind of thing that a second-year nurse would dress or a medical dresser. She smiled, faintly. It was like asking an electronics scientist to mend a domestic fuse. The scratches had dried under the coating of sprayed-on plastic sealant and it was possible to move freely under the soft folds of the pretty blouse. She walked with confidence down to the kitchen, remembering to take a tin of biscuits with her.

'So you'll have Peregrine Bradford back again. Did he seem any more attractive, meeting him informally, so to speak?' Wendy was showing an un-nerving interest in the episode.

'He was still in his off-duty clothes, I hardly recognised him,' said Rosalind. 'I thought he slept in a slick suit and highly polished Gucci shoes.'

'And now you know different? What *does* he sleep in, Ros?'

'I shall empty the milk jug over you if you tease me anymore. It was a highly . . . traumatic experience to be seen by him in a torn and very dirty shirt with my hair all over my eyes.' She tried to smile naturally, but wondered how difficult it would be to face him again in the theatre.

Two other sisters and a staff nurse wandered in and the conversation became general. It was a relief to sit with a half-filled cup of tea in her hand while the flow of talk left her room to breathe and think again about the unusual end to her game of tennis. A name penetrated her consciousness.

'Alan King was saying . . .' said one nurse.

'Is he back? He told me he was going out for the day. He was very full of himself, who's the new girl? Anyone I know?'

Wendy glanced at the frozen expression on Rosalind's face. 'No idea, probably tried it on and had the brush. Rosalind had to give him the elbow and I expect his new date stood him up.'

Rosalind shot a grateful look at her friend. In one sentence, she had told everyone that Alan had chased Rosalind and been repulsed, as if it had happened days ago and this date was something new. 'Poor man, he must be running out of possible talent, but he's coming to the concert tonight and he *is* quite fun to have around.'

'I went to a street market this morning,' said Rosalind, casually. 'In fact, Dr King gave me a lift as far as Charing Cross.' Her lips twitched with a repressed smile. 'He *was* all dressed up, come to think of it, but we didn't have time to talk as I'd missed my bus and the traffic took all his concentration.'

'Wonder where he was going?' said the nurse

who had mentioned him first. She looked disappointed and Rosalind knew that she had seen Alan King taking her to his car. What other people saw her leave? She recalled the empty windows overlooking the tennis courts. Empty and blind . . . but it would be natural for anyone with a room over-looking the courts to watch two attractive women playing tennis.

'Did you buy anything in the market?' said Wendy.

'I bought some china for an aunt who collects it and a rather good sweater, a few bits and pieces.' She shrugged.

Everyone now wanted to talk about bad bargains, good bargains and unusual items they had bought or nearly bought in such places and Rosalind slipped away to her room to bundle up the shirt securely and address it to Mr Bradford. She took it to the main entrance and handed it in to the porter. Under no circumstances could she force herself to return it to his room. If she escaped observation once, she knew better than to push her luck further in a hospital with eyes and ears everywhere.

The rest of the afternoon passed pleasantly and she washed the new china and found it was even prettier now that it had none of the market grime clinging to it. The disc bearing the sign of the Yin-Yang motif was like having an old friend returned, and she was sure that in no time she would accept the new pendant and forget that the other had existed. She smiled, the corners of her lips mobile with the irrepressible twitch of mirth that had been a source of trouble to her at school, in nursing lectures and most would-be serious situations in her life.

If Alan had the disc, he would wait until someone asked if anyone had seen it, and he must know it could belong to no-one but her as it had been left in her office, on her desk. 'He can just wait—and I'll wear the new one to confuse him further,' she murmured. She put the slender chain round her neck and felt the cold metal resting between her throat and cleavage. It was invisible, but gave her pleasure to think she was wearing it. The Yin and the Yang—forces of life, the intertwined symbol of life—of male and female, of love and sex. In a book, she had an illustration of the Pa Kua, the octagonal flat platter of broken and closed lines in a pattern showing the inescapable links of the past with the present and the future. It was compelling to read about such things and to wonder what her future would bring. The past was already hazy unless she was reminded of happenings, and the present was so close that she couldn't see it in its true dimensions. The further away the future stretched, the mistier it became. Would she still be content with her work in another five years? What of a home of her own? She was already having the simple desire to have somewhere to keep her belongings permanently . . . would she be happy alone in such a place?

For a moment, before she shut it out, slamming the door of her mind on the picture evoked, she saw an elegant but simple and very masculine room with a wolf-skin rug on the floor. She saw some rather tattered training shoes and a still damp waterproof jacket and felt again those firm fingers probing her scratches . . .

She had promised to carry some of the discs to the room used for the evening's entertainment and left her room soon after returning from supper. The small music room was already half full and an earnest-looking house surgeon was testing the record player. She took the discs and cassettes to him and joined Wendy, who sat about half way back in the centre. 'Does it get full?' she asked.

'Most of us like Chopin and it's quite a good way of meeting people who aren't completely hooked on disco-dancing and Pop. Not that I dislike either, but this is balm to my spirit,' said Wendy. 'And besides, although he's well and truly married with a family, we can watch Boris play and pant a little over him. He's the senior anaesthetist and took up playing to be a therapy for his hands. He gets rheumatism, not badly, but he has a horror of everything getting less supple. He's very good and plays with all the fire you'd expect from a Pole.'

'How old is he? I don't think I've met him.'

'You won't. He's strictly gynae and general. He's a contemporary of Perry Bradford. He and Slade and Boris were great buddies at one time—time and marriage split them a bit, but I expect the other two will be here this evening if they have no emergencies.'

'Both of them?'

'Well, Perry Bradford is back, or so I'm told.' Wendy giggled. 'I'd love to have seen you climbing in through his window.'

'Will you shut up?' Rosalind blushed. 'I hope to goodness that I wasn't seen if everyone here has the same kind of mind as you. He's probably forgotten it by now. I expect he lets young women through his room every hour on the hour.'

'And keeps them for longer than five minutes?' Her quizzical look was infuriating. 'Don't look now, but he's just come in with Slade and they're sitting at the back.'

Rosalind felt her back stiffen. She could imagine her scratches showing through the delicate material of her blouse. What if the half-sealed bleeding points oozed while the music was being played? She drew the light shawl that she'd brought with her over her back and shoulders, knowing she must appear strange to be covering up when every one in the room was shedding cardigans or jackets. A touch on her sore shoulder made her wince. 'I see there's a free place by you. Dare I flatter myself into thinking that you saved it for me?' Alan King's grinning face was within inches of her own. He was whispering as if they had a shared secret and, to anyone bothering to watch them, it must seem that she had saved the vacant seat for him and had a firm date for the concert.

'It's a free country,' she said, ungraciously.

'And even my touch makes you squirm.' He looked more hurt than annoyed. 'You nearly jumped a yard.'

'It isn't that. I scratched my shoulder and it's a bit sore.'

'Sunbathing already? That I would give much to see.'

'No, I played tennis and got caught on some wire.'

'*Je crois.*' His eyes were insolent.

'What do you mean?'

'Nothing . . . nothing at all. I was trying to remember in which room in the medical corridor was a room with barbed wire. I had a vision this afternoon. I was returning after a very abortive trip to London when I saw a lovely pair of legs vanishing along the corridor—just legs and a large sweat shirt—intriguing situation and very sexy. Had she or hadn't she anything on under that voluminous cover? Any time you want to borrow a shirt, I have a very good selection. I've always had the conviction that what is covered and merely hinted at is far more inflammable than nudity.'

'If you say another word, I'll leave. I see no reason why I should tell you anything. If you think you saw me, or someone like me, walking along a corridor after playing a game of tennis and quite rightly wearing a cover over brief tennis shorts, after taking a short cut looking for lost tennis balls, then I can't stop you jumping to the most bizarre conclusions! But if we are to get on, Dr King, I suggest you keep your fantasies to yourself.'

'I was only teasing,' he said, sulkily, but the sight of the flashing green eyes told him he had gone far enough. 'Now, who's here?' he said, to change the subject. He glanced round, waved to a couple of young doctors and saw the two men sitting at the back who were now joined by Boris Pilatz-check. 'The big guns . . . Pity about Boris,' he said.

Wendy bent towards him. 'What's that? Nothing wrong with him, is there?'

'No, worse luck. I shall have to go to another hospital if I want his kind of job. I'd like a change from ENT and he's good for a few years yet.'

'You talk as if he's an old man,' laughed Wendy. 'He's at the fascinating age. Just look back, Ros. Three really good-looking men with a bit of character and experience in their faces.'

'I'm younger than any of them,' said Alan.

'Get away! They're what? Ten years older than us? If I thought I'd have the ghost of a chance with any of them I'd lie down in front of their cars to get noticed.' She shrugged. 'But I never did like wasting time on married men.'

'Are they all married?' Rosalind tried to sound calm.

'Slade and Boris are and if a man as marvellous as the Peregrine isn't married, he must have someone somewhere in a love nest . . . or he may be still in love with the past.'

'He's a close devil,' said Alan King. There was a murmur and silence as the first piece of music was announced. Rosalind sat in a dream. The lovely, poignant music flowed round her, haunting and sad, tearing at the heart strings. Was he married . . . or had he a lover? The music changed to a Polonaise and Rosalind saw that the Polish doctor was seated at the grand piano. The music spoke of wild hopes and despair, defiance and sadness, and was followed by a burst of sincere and spontaneous applause. Many people left their seats for the interval and Wendy went to fetch coffee while Alan

King, suddenly embarrassed by the silence beside him, went to talk to another group of staff.

A soft touch on Rosalind's good shoulder made her turn. The serious face of Peregrine Bradford was full of apology. 'I'm very sorry, but can you tell me where Nurse Stephen would be? She isn't here and there's a possibility that Casualty can't cope with a child who has put something up his nose.'

'She may be out. I know that her boy friend was coming to London for a few days. I said that she needn't be on call tonight. I know I'm off, officially, until tomorrow morning, but I don't mind. If you need someone, I'll come.'

It was easy to talk of work and she was able to meet his gaze with no more than a flutter of her dark eyelashes to show that she was at all nervous. 'Have we time for coffee?'

'Oh yes, it isn't certain and it doesn't take much preparation. I just want to be sure that I can gather staff if and when needed. I see that you are with Alan—that makes it easier. If I know that I can find one of you, it follows that I shall find the other.' He left her staring after him. It isn't like that! she wanted to shout. He tried to kiss me in the office, against my will. He came to take this seat without being invited. He's nothing to me! A sick feeling in her heart told her that Peregrine Bradford couldn't have avoided seeing Alan bent over her, smiling intimately, showing that she wasn't cross with him for trying to kiss her. It only needs Alan to say that he took her up to Town and he would believe that they were much more than just good friends.

'What did Sir want?' Wendy handed her the plastic cup of coffee.

'We might have a case tonight,' said Rosalind. 'Nothing very much, but he'd need an anaesthetic.'

'I was hoping he was chatting you up.'

'Rubbish. You said he was married, didn't you?'

'No I didn't.' Wendy glanced at the flushed face and the bright green eyes. 'You don't know much about him, do you? And I'd say you were interested.'

'Not interested, just curious . . . quite different.'

'He had a girl friend when he was a student and she died. That's all I know. As far as I know, although I think that Anna and Slade know more, he hasn't bothered with women since then.'

'How did she die?'

'I couldn't find out. It was sudden and had to do with swimming. Might have drowned, must have done, she's dead.' She shrugged. 'Perhaps she had a weak heart and died of shock.'

Alan came back and Rosalind told him that they might be needed. 'Good,' he said. 'I can take you to the Falcon for a drink and a snack—they keep open very late in the Peregrine Bar—a kind of club membership to which I belong. We can leave the phone number and if they don't call us, we shall not have wasted our time.' He had recovered all his poise and his light brown eyes were once more full of approval as he looked at the soft draped blouse and the lightly folded shawl.

'Sorry . . . if we're needed it will be soon. The child is in Casualty now. If they can't get him to blow it down or take it from his nose we shall have to take him before he gets too frantic.'

As if that was a signal, Peregrine Bradford waved from the doorway and having attracted their attention, beckoned. They left the room quietly as the first lovely bars of a nocturne slipped across the air. 'Nocturne! Some hope we have of sleep,' said Alan, cheerfully. Rosalind knew there was no time to change her clothes but on reflection knew that all she needed to wear was an unsterile gown and mask and theatre cap over her ordinary clothes. The nose, being open to the outside air, could never be rendered sterile, only 'kitchen clean', and although the instruments would have to be boiled, as they were after all cases to prevent the spread of infection, they would be used by the surgeon held in his bare hands if there was no risk of infection either from surgeon to patient or from patient to any member of the theatre staff.

'What is it?' said Alan King.

'A child of six pushed a smooth pussy willow up his nose and they can't get it down. The pollen makes him sneeze badly and it might get pushed into a sinus if we can't get it out.'

'You sure you need me?'

'They've tried in Cas. and he's scared. The HS was a bit ham-handed and made the nose bleed.'

'When did he eat?'

'That's why we need you and Sister Mason. He had a meal just before it happened.'

'We'll need to wash out his stomach?' said Rosalind.

Alan King was suddenly alert and businesslike. 'We'd better do it thoroughly. I once saw a bead taken safely from a nose only to see it slip from the forceps into the bronchus. We don't want bronchoscopies as well as a simple removal of foreign body from nose.'

Rosalind smiled. If he could be like this all the time, she would value him as a friend and colleague. Peregrine Bradford saw the smile.

'How long do you need, Sister?' he said.

'No problem. Since I came here I make sure an emergency trolley is ready for such cases so that even if there was no SRN on duty, you would have everything ready. We had one case with Tony this week while you were away and it seemed a good idea.'

'Excellent.'

'I'll ring down for the child now, Mr Bradford,' she said.

'Thank you, Sister.' It was cool and formal . . . with none of the easy friendliness of the theatre during Tony Murray's sessions. It was obvious that Mr Peregrine Bradford had no intention of letting one slightly ridiculous encounter make him relax into informality during working conditions. He's forgotten it already, she thought, and forgot that only a few hours ago that was exactly what she had hoped he would do . . . forget that she had ever appeared in such an embarrassing condition.

'I'll put on a clean gown from the surgeon's room,' he said. The door was open and to her horror, Rosalind saw a parcel on the table.

'Christmas?' said Alan King, picking it up and reading the name. 'Someone loves you, Perry.'

'I wonder,' Mr Bradford solemnly pinched the

soft package. 'No, I don't think it's a token of love.'
He looked at Rosalind, wryly, and she blushed.
'It's of no importance,' he said and pushed it aside
to take up a white theatre gown.

Alan King refused to put on a gown. 'I suspect
that he'll be frightened of more white coats. I'll get
him under first.' Once more he was full of surprises.

'Good idea.' Peregrine Bradford put the gown
back on the table again. 'I ought to look at him
before we begin, so I'll come as I am.'

Rosalind watched the two men go into the anaesthetic room and close the door behind them. She
heard laughter as she brought the covered trolley
into the theatre and smiled. What child could be
scared of the good-looking, smiling doctors, dressed casually and surely not unlike members of the
little boy's family. She had caught only a glimpse of
the blue cotton shirt and the tight fitting cords of the
surgeon, far removed from the smartly-tailored
image he presented during his consultant's appoint-
ments, but very good, showing the tautness of firm
thighs and the strong line of his legs. The theatre
was warm when they brought the child in and laid
him gently on the table. Glyn Baker looked very
tiny in his white robe, very pale and with eyes
red with crying, she was overwhelmed by the
tenderness with which the tall surgeon took a swab
and cleaned away the tear stains before placing the
little head in the right position for examination.
The throat was blocked off, the stomach tube aspir-
ated so that no remnants of food could be inhaled
into the lungs if he was sick.

The smooth head of pussy willow was firmly

wedged and it took several minutes to loosen it and bring it out. Fragments came away and Rosalind did a kind of jig-saw puzzle on a dish to make sure that it was all there. A nasal douche sent the last of the particles down to the swab blocking off the throat and were sucked away, safely. The last inspection made, the throat pack was removed and Glyn lay looking deceptively angelic on the trolley.

'Look as if they could sprout wings when they're like that,' said Alan, 'but I believe he's a devil at home. He's been in with a broken arm already, and a badly cut foot when he ran about with no shoes on his feet, and he had infantile excema when he was a baby. He also swears like a trooper.'

'Well, we've done what we can—let's hope he's had enough of this hospital and learns to avoid injury in future.' Peregrine Bradford regarded his patient with a smile. 'Make quite a useful scrum half later.'

'Do you still play?' said Alan as the porter and nurse came for the patient and case chart. Rosalind brought coffee which had been simmering in a jug in a small instrument steriliser.

'Of course, not quite past it yet,' said the surgeon. He slipped out of his gown. 'Do you?'

'No, much too rough. Who plays from Beattie's? I must come and watch when you get a match with St Mary's.' His face was free of guile but Rosalind had the absurd suspicion that he was trying to find out who on the medical corridor owned a certain vast rugby sweat shirt with BEATTIE'S across the front and back. He glanced at Rosalind and grinned, knowingly. 'Rough lot, these rugby types, Ros.'

'I didn't know that I'd given permission for you to call me that,' she said. But only Alan heard. The surgeon had walked away to the surgeon's room with his coffee cup in his hand, leaving Rosalind with the tray and the remaining cups.

She handed a cup to Alan King. 'Take it in there with him. I'm drinking mine while I work.'

'We could have it together in the office. I think he was being tactful, don't you?'

'He was being stand-offish, that's all. I have work to do and I would like to get the theatre clear by midnight.' She stalked away, her fair hair glinting in the light as she removed her theatre cap. She stood by the sink, and the long gown grew damp as the taps splashed into the deep basin. She took off the gown as soon as the wet work was done and sat on the anaesthetist's stool while she finished her coffee and dried the instruments. It was odd to be sitting on a revolving stool wearing high-heeled shoes and sheer stockings, a deep blue velvet skirt and a pretty blouse delicately embroidered with tiny flowers. Her hair, tied back in a pony tail to keep it away from her face, was secured by a velvet bow the same colour as the skirt, and as Peregrine Bradford came back into the theatre to find the wrist watch he'd placed on a shelf, he paused for a minute until Rosalind sensed that she was being watched, uncrossed her long legs and swung down from the stool.

'Thank you for your help,' he said. He stared at her and she wished she had changed into uniform or at least kept the gown on while she finished her work. He must think her slack and unprofessional, even if one made allowances for the fact that she had volunteered her services. 'And thank you for the parcel,' he said. She found her pulses racing as Alan came silently behind the surgeon and listened.

'Thank you,' she said, softly, hoping that Alan couldn't hear. 'Would you or Dr King like more coffee?' She looked beyond him and Mr Bradford realised that they weren't alone. He turned. 'No, I think you've done enough for one night, Sister.'

Alan King lounged against the table. 'I'll help you put away the instruments if you like,' he said.

'I'd rather like you to look in on Glyn Baker. He might need a tranquilliser and you know what he's had. Would you write him up for whatever he needs?' The voice was bland but with hidden steel somewhere in the depths of the well-modulated tones. Alan King walked away without another word and the outer door swung furiously as he left.

'Glyn will be discharged tomorrow?'

'Yes, there's nothing wrong with him.'

'I'll pop the bits in a jar—he'll enjoy boasting to his friends. We gave up giving tonsils as some of the little horrors broke the jars, and even if they are in formaldehyde, infected tonsils aren't quite suitable as playthings, are they? I'll seal this jar and I think it will stand up to even little Glyn Baker.'

She was talking rapidly and, she suspected, talking a lot of nonsense. He walked through into the sterilising room. Everything was in place and shining clean. 'No list tomorrow. I have two lectures to give. One to students and one for the final-year nurses. I wonder if I could borrow a few basics that Tony isn't using?'

Rosalind blushed. It was an order, but said much more pleasantly than the first time he had demanded instruments, and been so cross with her when she refused him.

'I'll make a list if you'll come into the office,' she said. 'We have a short list for Mr Murray early tomorrow. Nurse can pack a bag from the list after we've finished.' He nodded. 'We can then check both ways,' she said. He smiled slightly and she knew he was labelling her a thoroughly fussy theatre sister. But at least he had been satisfied with her help tonight. She sat at the desk and drew a clean sheet of paper towards her. She raised her head, pen poised and was disconcerted by the intent gaze of the deep blue eyes, made more blue by the colour of his shirt. Another thing made her look again at his shirt. From the neck peeped a chain, such as some men wear to carry identity discs or more ornamental pendants. She couldn't see what hung on the chain but the chain was slender, indicating something quite light in weight. She could feel the chain of her own disc catching again, and remembered that she had worn it and forgotten to remove it before coming to the theatre.

Some men wore a form of good luck charm, given them by girl friends, or things worn in memory of lost friends. He might well have a keepsake . . . a talisman from the girl he had loved and lost. He still loves her and wears her token in remembrance, she thought. She glanced at the still, strong face and the wings of dark hair tinged with grey just at the temples while the rest of his hair shone thickly and dark. He was so handsome and so remote, so unattainable except to have some share in his professional life. I used to laugh at sisters who fell in love with doctors and served them with devotion even if they knew they could never be loved in the way a woman wants to be loved, and now, I'm doing just that. I'll have to change my job. It was almost a physical shock to make the discovery that she could not work with him for much longer knowing that his nearness threatened her concentration on her work, her self control and the possibility of her ever loving any other man while he was there.

He dictated the list and she made suggestions for the nurses' lecture, knowing the shortcomings of many doctors who speak to nurses and tell them all the wrong things and leave out the essentials. 'Are you telling me that we give bad lectures?' he said. His eyes glinted with something less than anger and more than mere interest.

'I've never heard you lecture, Mr Bradford, but I know one or two consultants who talk down to nurses and leave them with no real instruction.'

'I shall have to let you see my lectures some time, Sister. Perhaps you could come to my room and we could go over a few things.'

'You could bring your notes here, sir.'

'Yes . . . so I could. It's quite cosy and almost private in here.' She felt her heart beating faster with a mixture of rage and helplessness. He was goading her about that time when Alan had tried to kiss her. She bent her head so that he wouldn't see the trembling lips. A hand closed over her own. 'Don't misunderstand me, I was not referring to Alan. I just wondered if your back needed some attention before tomorrow. May I examine your scratches, Sister?'

His voice and manner were formal. 'Of course, if you think it necessary,' she said. She turned away and pulled her shirt out of the tight waistband, dragging it high over her back. She felt his fingers trace the edge of a scar and shuddered. 'I'm sorry . . . I'm hurting you.'

'No,' she breathed, her eyes closed. Oh, God! Let me keep my cool. The blood pounded in her brain and his hands were a caress that made her want him and want him and . . . want him.

He pulled down the shirt and his voice was rough and deep. 'Everything fine . . . it will be clear in a day or so.' She stood, tucking in the shirt ends, awkwardly. The waistband was tight and if she had been alone she would have undone the zip and the top button before tucking away the excess material. 'It's crooked,' he said. His hands tweaked the shirt and lined it up correctly. He undid the top button and she pushed the shirt under the waistband, not daring to look up.

A slight movement above her that could have been a draught, a bird's wing or a dream, told her that his lips had touched the back of her neck where the thick swathe of honey-gold hair fell sideways revealing the tender nape that looked like the neck of a child.

He turned her to face him and she was in a tight and urgent embrace. He kissed her on the mouth and she saw his eyes full of pain. As suddenly, he thrust her away. 'Never wear civilian clothes in the theatre again . . . it's unprofessional.' The outer door swung several times after he had gone. She put a hand to her breast where something hard had dug into the soft flesh. The talisman that he was wearing was full of pain, full of sorrow, and she wept as she remembered that he had kissed her in a moment of desperation for his lost love, and she could have been any woman who was near and feminine enough to move him to desire.

CHAPTER SEVEN

'How is the last stapedectomy and prosthesis?'

'You mean Andrew Young?' Sister Rosalind Mason smiled to herself in the darkened theatre. The slight friction between the surgeon, Mr Peregrine Bradford and his anaesthetist Dr Alan King was niggling away again. It was well known that Peregrine Bradford had a bee in his bonnet about using the right names for people and, as yet, Rosalind had never known him to forget a patient's name. He was always meticulous in his use of names and, true to the traditions of the hospital, the habit was catching and Rosalind found herself checking that her staff used names and didn't refer to cases as cases.

'I suppose so . . . the one you did two weeks ago.' Alan King tried to sound off-hand, but he knew that he was slack about such things and suspected that the surgeon had heard the story that had followed him to Beattie's, of the time when he had forgotten a name and the wrong patient was written up for the wrong treatment. No harm had been done as the treatment was not given, but tales like that follow people and do no good for their reputations.

'Andrew Young went home yesterday, very pleased with himself and us.' The surgeon looked intently through the eye-piece of the microscope and concentrated on carving out a tiny window in the over-growth of bone that was causing progressive deafness in a fairly young woman. 'Now, Mrs Dora Bright will go home wondering why she put off coming to see us for so long. I think she'll be lucky enough to get away with this operation alone as the rate of thickening seems to have slowed down and although we'll obviously check on her condition in future, this will improve the situation.'

His hand went out in the darkness to the dimly seen square of cloth on which a cross of white tape was sewn to the green cotton, dividing it into four smaller squares. The tiny pair of forceps with minute points took a snippet of finely-woven gauze plugging which lay with others like it in one of the squares. Rosalind had dipped the small swabs in Adrenaline 1:1000 solution to be used to control any bleeding from the site of operation. In another square were wisps of cotton wool taken from a sterile blob of the material and rolled between the sterile gloved fingers of whoever was scrubbing for the operation. These were dry and he now took one to mop up the blood and Adrenaline left in the aperture. The oozing stopped and he waved aside the miniscule pellet of sterile wax that the theatre sister offered to him. Bleeding from bone can never be tied off neatly as blood vessels in soft tissue can be controlled, but pressure and sealing with wax are used in many operations on the ear and mastoid process.

'Good,' he said and began to bring the operation to an end. 'She'll do, Alan,' he said, with more warmth. 'Rather a good team effort, I thought.'

There was a slow handclap from the observation gallery, and he grinned up at the dark glass-fronted room. 'When you can do as good . . . I'll clap you, too.'

The patient was swiftly taken down to the ward, neatly bandaged and almost awake. 'She was very relaxed about the whole thing . . . I needed only a very light anaesthetic for her,' said Alan King. The lights were on again between cases and the theatre staff blinked in the sudden brightness. Peregrine Bradford tore off his gloves and stretched. Alan King threw the intra-trachial tube into the bin and asked for more swabs for his trolley. A junior nurse swabbed the floor area round the table and the sound of metal on metal told of the instruments used for the last case being carefully washed before being sterilised again.

Rosalind went to the scrubbing-up bay and put her used gown into the shute before scrubbing for the third time that afternoon.

After a week of routine lists, today had been full and a slight strain, having three major cases all done by Peregrine Bradford. She slumped her shoulders after the tension of being alert in the darkened theatre for long periods, having to antici-pate the needs of a man working in the dark, from her point of view, using only his headlight and the built-in light of the microscope. It was a relief to find that once he was working, no other influence could affect him and any embarrassment that she might feel when his deep blue eyes regarded her with their mockery, disapproval or humour, was forgotten. I enjoy working with him, she thought. I am all thumbs as soon as the list is over, but I can cope as far as our working relationship goes.

'Ready, Sister?' She nodded and turned away, aware of the eyes above the mask and the sense of his nearness. He threw down his used gown and the junior nurse picked it up. As she turned away, Rosalind saw that under the Tee-shirt he wore with theatre trousers, he was wearing the chain and pendant round his neck again. She busied herself getting her sterile trolley ready and ceased to wonder why he wore the Tee-shirt as he was usually complaining that he was too hot wearing anything but a theatre gown and trousers. Surely he wasn't self-conscious about wearing so little? Most surgeons pleased themselves and the average nurse was used to men in every stage of undress and blinked not an eyelid at the sight of the hairy chests, spare tyres of fat or pallid stomachs revealed—and they rather enjoyed seeing such lovely beef-cake as Slade Forsythe, or Peregrine Bradford, stripped down to the waist.

The last case, a mastoidectomy, was wheeled in and the boy of eight was found to have a badly-infected mastoid process. Rosalind glanced at the house surgeon who was assisting, and wondered if he would be all right, but he smiled at her as if to say he was over his first dread of hearing and seeing bone tissue removed. The cavity was plugged and bandaged and the trolley pushed away from the operating table. The telephone rang.

Peregrine Bradford came back and said, 'Hold it, Alan. There's a child with otitis media—it won't take a second. I told them to bring her in.'

'Myringotomy set, Nurse!' called Rosalind.

'Thank you, Sister,' said Peregrine. She noticed that he looked tense for the first time during the long and arduous list.

'Make sure there's plenty of coffee, Nurse, everyone will need some after this list . . . including you.' The junior smiled and pushed back a wisp of hair that had escaped from under her cap. She knew that junior staff were not allowed coffee in the theatre unless invited by the sister in charge and was grateful for an understanding senior.

The little girl was wheeled in, looking drowsy with drugs, but she still moaned and swung her head from side to side to shake off the pain. Alan King stood with a face mask, ready to give her a whiff of anaesthetic, enough to make her insensible to the slight operation.

'What are we going to do, Nurse?' asked the surgeon.

'You are going to make a tiny incision in the tympanic membrane, or drum of the ear, because there is a mass of fluid or pus pressing on it from the middle ear.'

He laughed. 'Right first time . . . straight out of a text book, or from Sister?'

'Sister told me,' said the junior.

'And you remembered.' He washed his hands and stood where the child couldn't see the small blade on the angled handle. He wore a headlight and in his other hand had an auroscope to insert in the outer ear and show the drum clearly. He nodded to Alan King, who held the mask over the child's face lowering it on to the face for a minute only when her eyes fell shut, so that she didn't feel the mask on her until the fumes had made her unconscious.

Rosalind held the small head firmly while the incision was made and the released discharge flowed freely. 'Why did I do that instead of allowing the drum to burst, as it might do if left?' he said.

'It will leave no scar if you incise, but if it burst, the scar would be uneven and extensive,' said the nurse.

Rosalind sensed the mocking smile as he said, 'I see that Sister will have to give you your lectures.'

'Anyone off for Easter? You aren't planning a marathon theatre session are you, Perry?' Alan King looked round at the staff.

'No . . . we've no more fenestrations planned until the Dutch contingent come next month to watch the ones I'm doing here and a couple of private ones. I heard that you were standing in for Boris.'

'Yes, I'm not going away. Are you, Sister?' The light brown eyes were speculative. Rosalind bristled. He had asked her the same question before the list started and she had told him that she was going on holiday in two months and wanted to save up a few days to tag on to the end so that she could go on a package to Greece.

'As I told you when you asked me before the list, I am not due for any holiday yet and I have people to see in London!' The last phrase she added for good measure, knowing that he was rather hoping Peregrine Bradford and the rest of the staff would think they had something planned together. 'I believe Sister Fletcher is off, if you want to keep tabs on staff activities,' she said. She caught a gleam in the blue eyes of the surgeon and did she imagine it or did he wink at her? He was less tense now that the child had gone.

'What would happen if the infection wasn't taken away or didn't respond to drugs, Sir?' said the junior who was eager to learn.

He looked at her with eyes suddenly dark. 'Encephalitis, meningitis . . . death if the infection reached the covering of the brain.' He seemed to drag his thoughts back from something menacing. 'But it never happens, with modern drugs and early diagnosis.' He smiled, bleakly, 'Well, hardly ever.'

'The little girl will be all right?'

'Oh yes . . . we'll leave it to discharge and then dry up the ear with spirit vini meth drops. She'll feel much better at once now that the pressure has been released. In her case, she had a bad attack of measles and this is sometimes a complication, but it's soon over when treated as we have done.'

'Coffee? Or we can manage tea?' Rosalind smiled at a point midway between the two men.

'Do you have anything to eat here? I have to see patients before dinner and I'm starving.' Peregrine Bradford smiled and her heart did strange acrobatics. The sweetness of a man's mouth as it relaxes from stern repose was something of which she had never guessed the power.

'I wondered, as it was such a long list,' she said, and brought a plate of buns and biscuits into the surgeon's room, with sandwiches begged from the kitchen.

'You'll join us? This is wonderful,' said Peregrine, taking two sandwiches.

'I'll come in later,' she said. 'I must see that the more delicate instruments are back in their boxes first.' He nodded and took another sandwich and she went to see what was happening in the sterilising room. Absentmindedly, she scratched her back where the healed lines of scars itched as they peeled. It seemed an age since the day when he had cleaned her back and tended it so gently, an age since he had checked on his own work and then kissed her in sadness and a kind of frustrated fury. She checked the instruments, not intending to go back to the men. She drank coffee from a mug as she put the last box away and went to her office to change into uniform while the nurses went to supper.

There was silence in the other rooms of the unit and she thought that they had left through the outer doors. The theatre gleamed damply and there was no list for the next day as no child wanted to be in hospital at Easter unless it was absolutely necessary. It should be slack and possibly boring, but I might as well be here, on duty half of the time with Nurse Stephen taking the other half. Where would I go if I was off? But she knew that she had only to lift a telephone and ring one of half a dozen old friends to be welcomed with enthusiasm. Why then had the thought lost all flavour? As if life began and ended with Beattie's . . . or with one moody-eyed surgeon who thought of her as a young, empty-headed girl with ideas above her position. But he was pleasant today . . . and we do get on, professionally, she thought.

She adjusted the bow under her chin and heard the nurses returning from supper. One of them had worked for a part of her off-duty and so Rosalind sent her off at once. The other nurse lived in and was told to go to the Nurses' Home and be on call until the usual time for going off duty. Rosalind rang down to the children's ward.

'Sister Fletcher here.'

'It's Ros. How is little Sally?'

'The ear's discharging nicely . . . all over the pillow. She's had the dressing off twice, but she's feeling good.'

'Have a good holiday. Meant to ring you earlier, but we've been up to our eyes.'

'You know you offered to lend me a swim suit? Can I take it from your room?'

'I left it on the bed, help yourself. It should be interesting . . . be good.'

'I hope not,' said Wendy and rang off.

Rosalind smiled and was still smiling when she looked up and saw Peregrine Bradford standing in the doorway. 'You didn't join us for coffee,' he said, accusingly.

'I was held up,' she said. 'Did you eat all the sandwiches?'

'I'm afraid we did. Have you eaten?'

'I had coffee while I worked and I can get something in the dining room now.' She picked up her belt and put it on. She sensed his eyes examining her face and fumbled with the buckle, looking down as she did so. 'I rang Children's. Little Sally is fine . . . leaking joyfully.' She laughed. 'The ward is to be closed for a few days while Sister Fletcher is away, so we shall be very slack if you aren't working here. Sister goes tonight and when the last three children go home on Saturday, the ward will be closed.'

'Where's she going?' He stood in her way as she made towards the door. She tried to be composed while her pulse rate exceeded the speed limit. If only he'd look stern and forbidding again she could cope with her own emotions and even generate a little hate, but now, as he sat on the chair by the door, looking slightly tired, but friendly, she wanted to go to him and make him rest in her arms.

'She belongs to a society that visits Roman remains. They don't dig, but study history and look at the artefacts that other people dig up.'

'Sounds fascinating,' he said, cryptically.

'They have social events too. They visited Bath last year and had a Roman evening there, in the right clothes, eating the right foods and swimming in the Roman Baths.' She wrinkled her brow. 'At least they wanted to swim there but had to make do with the new sport's complex baths as the Roman Baths were closed due to a bug they found in the water there.'

'I heard about it.' His face was grim as if the mention of something she'd said touched him deeply. 'Where is she now?' It was shot at her as if she was responsible for the movements of the sister from the children's ward.

'I think they'll have better luck this year. They've found a small spa in good condition that belonged to one of the Stately Homes. It's only possible to visit by appointment and the baths themselves have only just been opened to the few who now see it. It should be rather good, all those guests in togas or whatever, swimming in warm spa water as they did long ago.'

'Where is she?'

'It's the spa dedicated to Minerva, discovered a few years ago when they dug for foundations.'

'They have no right to let people swim there—has it been given a clean bill of health?'

She stepped backwards, alarmed. His face was contorted with sorrow and fury. 'I . . . suppose so.'

'You suppose . . . you suppose? Where is this place, this cesspool of infection?'

'But it's a pool of spa water, bubbling out of the earth and full of health-giving minerals . . . isn't it?' He gripped her arms, hurting her. 'I don't know the address, it can't be that important . . . the authorities would never allow swimming in an infected pool, not after finding that bug in the Roman Baths at Bath.'

He released his grip. 'You're right, of course.' He swallowed hard. 'Just promise me that you'll never swim in a place like that, promise.'

'I promise, if you feel so strongly about it, but I can't see that it's any concern of yours, Mr Bradford.'

'No . . . forgive me.' He walked away, leaving her staring after him and wondering what storm lay under that dark clouded brow. She went down to the dining room but was too tired to eat the rather unappetising food. She drank more coffee and went back to the theatre to finish writing the notes and to tidy her desk. It was peaceful, sitting all alone with the faint sounds of the theatre sifting through the stillness. She checked the settings for emergencies, made sure that the cupboards were locked and rang down to the lodge for a porter to take drums to the auto-clave for sterilising. There were many small jobs to be done when the theatre was not in use. The past week had been busy, but she felt a sense of great satisfaction that all the cases had gone well.

The dim light in the observation gallery was on and she went to turn it off and to make sure that no student had left notes, pens or anything he might want when the theatre was not in use and the gallery was locked. She climbed the steps and went in, picked up a notebook and pen and a text book, ready to leave in her office where they could be taken by the owners. She hesitated, thinking she saw a movement in the theatre. Being now in darkness, she couldn't be seen from below and she watched Alan King move towards her office, throw open the door and stride in. She smiled as he came out again, more slowly, his disappointment apparent. He left the theatre and she could see how cross he was that she had avoided him. 'I wonder what he wanted?' she said aloud, as she went back through the main theatre to put out the light in her office.

'Didn't you want to find out?' She started back, a cry on her lips. 'I'm sorry. Perhaps I should have come sooner and you could have hidden from me, too.' Peregrine Bradford glanced at the dark gallery and grinned. 'I assume that you were skulking up there?'

'I never skulk,' she said, with dignity, but the corners of her mouth gave her away. 'I went to put out the light and saw Dr King go through the theatre. When I came down, he had gone.'

'And you hurried down, only to find you were too late?' He sounded almost anxious to know that she *was* avoiding Alan King.

'I could ring him to find out what he wanted,' she said.

'Before you do . . . I have a message.'

'Not a case? I think we've all done enough for one day. Oh, was that why he came up? To tell me that there was a case?'

'No, I think he wanted to make sure you were going to be . . . available.'

'What message, Mr Bradford?'

'Anna and Slade Forsythe asked me to say that they are having one of their impromptu parties tonight. It's very close to the hospital and we can leave a phone number.'

'We?' She almost whispered it.

'This is no district for young girls to walk about on their own at night. It is too near to warrant a taxi or a car, so I am offering my services as escort for the evening.' He smiled. 'There comes a time when tiredness is something best beaten by getting tired another way. I'm tired, you're tired and I expect that everyone there is tired, but a change will refresh us, and you've earned a change—thank you for today.' He smiled again, politely. 'If you can be changed in half an hour, I'll be at the entrance of the Nurses' Home.' He went before she could say she had another date, she had to wash her hair, she was much too tired . . . or any of the excuses that were usual when a girl didn't wish to take up an invitation. But she wanted to go, even if he was being polite and passing on the invitation from Anna.

He couldn't do anything *but* ask to take me if we're to go to the same party, she thought as she took a quick shower. On an impulse, she took a loosely-cut shirt of pale grey panné velvet with a simple tie at the neck but extravagant sleeves and a drawstring waist that could be tied at the natural waistline, on the hips or let fall as a smock. It was something she had made from a couturier pattern and had seldom worn, but it looked right with tightly-fitting black silk trousers and velvet mules. Regretfully, she put the mules away as looking too much like bedroom wear, and wore high-heeled black sandals which showed off the delicate arch to her feet. It was all very neat and restrained, but the opulence of the material was stunning. As she brushed her hair, she wondered if she had taken too much care over her appearance, and caught the honey locks back with deep set combs of pale grey, giving the illusion of the efficient theatre sister lurking under the beautiful shirt.

I might as well wear it, she convinced herself. I have little enough opportunity for such things and if this is an informal evening, with everyone lounging around and talking, it will be comfortable and warm and will show that I thought the party worth a little trouble.

'Nice timing.' Peregrine Bradford looked down at her and saw only the disciplined hair and the plain dark coat she wore over her shirt and trousers. He smiled. 'I see you've brought some food . . . always welcome and it's too much to expect Anna to supply for a crowd.'

'I brought some wine, too. I had some left from a party I gave when I left my last job and it was too good to leave behind.' She saw that he carried a stout paper bag from a leading West End caterer. 'You must have known about this,' she said.

'No, it was all very sudden. Anna was off duty and Slade was free . . . we aren't all that busy and some of the others are emptying wards for Easter. I have the advantage of a fridge in my room with a freezer compartment on top. I keep a few things for occasions such as this.' He laughed. 'Let's hope it's all thawed out, unless you fancy eating pâté ice lollies?'

She relaxed. He had changed from the strangely furious man who had demanded to know where Wendy was going for the Roman weekend. If the evening could be like this, with him adopting a slightly bantering tone, she could survive and perhaps forget the impact of his slightest touch. There would be others at the party. 'It sounds . . . different.' She laughed. 'Do I know anyone going? I've met Anna and she introduced me to Slade, but I haven't met many people other than theatre staff.'

He told her several names, of physicians, the casualty officer and some registrars that Rosalind knew by sight or had met when she visited the wards. He made no mention of Alan King and she hoped that he wouldn't be there.

'What about Tony Murray?'

'He doesn't come to many parties. He's a family man, lucky devil, and swans off home at the drop of a hat.' He paused, as if making an effort to say something on his mind. 'You call him Tony . . . could you bear to use my first name, if only on these occasions?' She glanced up, startled, and blushed, blessing the peculiar light cast on them by the street lamps that hid any colour. 'You also call King by his first name, so would it not be possible?'

'Of course, if you want me to. The others . . . it came naturally, I mean they seemed to expect it and we are roughly at the same stage of seniority . . . I mean . . . they took it for granted and so did I.'

He gave a short, humourless laugh. 'That's quite the most tactful way of telling me that they are in your age group and I am too old.'

'Oh, no, I said seniority and I mean that, you are not too old . . . you must know that half of the nursing staff think you the most attractive man at Beattie's.' She heard the words fall from her lips and couldn't stop them.

They reached a thick oak door in the front of a rather ugly house. 'And the other half . . . Rosalind?' He rang the bell. 'I wonder to which half you belong.' He was smiling sadly. 'Hello Anna, we're not late, are we?' he said with a complete change of tone. They went in and he thrust the package into the hands of his hostess. Rosalind followed her into a bedroom where she could leave her coat and was glad that she had dressed up a little. Anna wore a long caftan of glowing colours that set off her lovely features. She smiled and took the wine and biscuits.

'I couldn't get anything more interesting,' said Rosalind.

'This is marvellous. We've enough food for an army and everyone seems to have brought wine or cider. I love your shirt . . . must have cost the earth.' She brushed her hand against the soft, slinky material. 'Very sexy, better not sit with Alan wearing that or he'll never keep his hands to himself.'

'Oh . . . he's not here?'

'He might look in. I mentioned the party, but he thought he had another date tonight.'

'Thank goodness for that. Perhaps he'll bring his date along.'

Anna gave her a searching glance. 'Don't be too optimistic. He's been hinting for a long time that he hoped to make it with you.'

'Well, he can forget it. I thought I'd made that quite clear.'

'I'm glad,' said Anna, with a smile that concealed something faintly pleasing. 'Pity that Wendy couldn't come. Where is she, by the way? I had no time to talk to her this week. She's away and that's all I know.'

'She's gone on a Roman weekend, at a place where they discovered a Roman spa and have made a feature of the hot baths. It should be fun.' She watched the growing unease in Anna's face. 'What is it? What's wrong with her going there?'

'Does Perry know?'

'Yes, I told him and he acted very oddly. Please, Anna, tell me what's going on.'

'Look . . . I'm glad you mentioned this and I'll tell you about it later, but don't mention it again to Perry. Excuse me . . . that's the bell again . . . mingle and I'll introduce you if Perry hasn't already done so when I'm free.'

Diffidently, Rosalind walked into the huge sitting room where a group of people were talking and laughing and Slade was pouring drinks for newcomers. She accepted a glass of white wine and he drew her into the circle. It was warm and friendly and she sank on to an enormous sag-bag of crimson velvet. The young physician on her right made a very funny remark and she joined in the laughter. She sensed rather than saw that Peregrine had come into the room and hated herself for over-reacting as if he had touched her. 'Goose walking over your grave?' said her neighbour.

'Something like that,' she said, and tried to smile normally. She looked up and saw him staring at her. She saw him take the glass of wine offered to him and come to her side. Her heart was beating like a muffled bell but she was a little more confident. He had looked at her not as a surgeon regarding the efficiency or otherwise of his theatre sister, not as a man seeing a girl looking a mess and disgracing herself, but as a woman who looked attractive and merited a second glance. She took a sip from her glass. It was a party. Here, she was just a girl who hoped to enjoy the company of all these nice people, so why not make the most of everything even if it all faded away as soon as the party was over? 'There's room for one here,' she called, and he came to sit beside her on the enormous cushion.

'You look . . . full of the party spirit,' he said, but she knew that he had begun to say something different.

'How is it that the surgeons get all the pretty sisters?' asked Charles Bing, the physician on her other side.

'It takes a special kind of intelligence to make a good theatre sister . . . how can we help it if they're good to look at?' Rosalind laughed. 'It's true,' Peregrine continued. 'I was thinking how lovely our hostess looks tonight.'

'But the physicians are friendlier and say more pretty speeches without having their arms twisted,' said Rosalind, softly.

'Come and eat, I know you're starving or you would take a compliment when it was offered.'

'I thought it a little second-hand,' she said, but let him haul to her feet. She held her glass in one hand and rose unsteadily from the cushion that gave under her and offered no support. He held her as she regained her balance and his arm went round the silken waist. His grip was firm and safe and through her velvet shirt the warmth of her bosom met the male hardness of his chest. She stepped aside and he led her to the kitchen where a long table was covered with dishes and plates of food. His hand lingered on her shoulder as he pointed out the pâté he had brought and reached for the dish and slices of French bread. They took the food to a window seat on the first low landing of the stairway and looked down at the hall that was rapidly filling with hospital staff in jeans, in smart clothes, in whatever they wanted to wear. It all looked right, as relaxed talk and laughter floated up to the pair watching and eating the very good food.

Anna came to the foot of the stairs and smiled up at them. Rosalind thought she looked anxious, but her brow cleared when Peregrine complimented her on the success of the party. At first, they were both too hungry to bother with polite conversation, but at last, as coffee scents came from the kitchen, Peregrine took the empty plates and went in to see what there was that might fill the last gaps. He came back with a tray of coffee and gateau which he put on the window seat between them. 'You're not eating all that?' Rosalind smiled. This was a new side to the man who scared her and embarrassed her and fascinated her.

'Not all of it. It's a relief to know that you are fond of good food. I can't bear women who pick at food and waste it.'

'Two compliments in one evening . . . or one and a half?'

'Eat up and stop being cheeky.'

'You sound like my school master.' She bit her lip. Once more she had hinted that he was not of her generation, when she had never felt closer to him.

He seemed not to have noticed, but his blue eyes were sad. 'Do you know when Wendy is due back?' he said.

'Wendy?' The question had come suddenly, out of nothing.

'I want to get in touch with her as soon as she returns.'

'She will be away for two days and then she's going to her parents for the other two days. I don't know her address.'

He looked sombrely into his glass. 'Let me get you more wine,' he said, as if shaking off a dark and sinister thought. He grabbed her glass and went down to the sitting room. Rosalind wondered if he was tired of her company and was making an excuse to leave her, but he reappeared in a minute with more drinks.

'What's wrong, Perry?' she asked, quietly, the wine and the friendly house giving her courage to speak to him as she would to any other man on the staff who she knew slightly.

'Wrong?' He brooded and the blue eyes were grey with the same pain she had seen earlier. 'Nothing is wrong, but the past never leaves one alone.'

The past . . . that dark shadow that she could never share and never erase even if she grew close to him. 'What is it?' She forgot that this was the man who could bring her to the edge of desire with a touch. He was a man in trouble, and needed comfort, as much as a patient would do when there were dark thoughts to be fought. She put a hand on his arm and looked up into the darkened eyes with great green pools of brightness, and the wide sweep of her sleeve lay softly on his bare wrist.

'I lost a very good friend because she swam in contaminated water.'

'Oh . . . how terrible.'

He smoothed the soft velvet with one finger. 'You told me that Wendy was going to swim in a hot spring that has been open for such a short time that it can't have been examined for organisms, or not to a very high degree of certainty. It all came flooding back and I value the lives of healthy people too much to want them wasted by accident.'

'What happened?' she said, through dry lips. It was horrible to think of anyone dying of such a thing, but that wasn't the reason for her sorrow. He was still in love with a girl who had died tragically and left him with a memory that rightly or wrongly enshrined her in his heart for ever. There'll never be room for another woman, she thought. She had a sudden vision of a girl of her own age giving him a keepsake, as American youth exchange Fraternity badges with Sorority badges in college. Her gaze went to the thin chain round his neck. 'And you wear the talisman from the girl you loved on that chain.' She said it softly, without expression, hardly knowing that he heard. This glimpse of the man he could be when the traumas of his exacting work were relaxed was the one tiny leaf from his tree of life that she would ever see and possess, and the leaf was already withering. He would never forget that nameless girl.

'Yes,' he said, with a slightly quizzical expression. 'I carry the talisman of the girl I love on this chain. It is all I have and it remains hidden from view.'

'Is that why you didn't strip off in the theatre?' she said, without thinking.

'How observant you are, Sister,' he mocked, and

the tension was broken. The evening continued with Anna coming to break up groups so that they could re-form to meet new faces and it was another two hours before Rosalind found herself near to Peregrine again. She laughed and was bright and witty, but under her façade of mirth lay a cold film of misery. He hadn't said it was a talisman from the girl he had loved, he said he still loved her. 'The girl I love . . .' he'd said.

At midnight, Alan King came by to call in and have a glass of wine. He looked round the room and saw Rosalind talking to Charles Bing who was trying to interest her in his fishing tales. Alan made his way through the tangle of chairs and cushions and touched her arm. 'Well, hello . . . you look like a beautiful being from outer space with all that silvery grey . . . I'm glad I came.'

They regarded him with less than enthusiasm and he sat watching them as he sipped his drink. 'Nice party,' said Rosalind. She fiddled with the chain round her neck. Since her conversation with Peregrine, she had been conscious of the medallion resting on her bare flesh. He wore one too, but his was a gift of love. She tried to think of something witty to say to Alan but could only listen to the ramblings of Charles Bing.

'Why don't you take it off if it worries you?' said Alan.

She fished it out over the narrow collar and examined it. Contrary to the sensations it had caused this evening, it was *not* red hot and looked as it had done when she fixed it earlier. Alan looked at it as it dangled on the front of her shirt. 'Yin and

Yang?' He raised an eyebrow and her lips twitched. He was surprised and she knew why. He had taken her original disc from her desk top in her office and he must wonder where she had obtained another . . . or worse still, he would begin to think he'd taken the property of another member of the theatre staff!

'Very popular,' she said.

'And very meaningful,' he said. 'Where have I seen one just like it?' He appeared to think deeply. 'I know.' He stared at her as if very surprised and she was impressed by his acting. 'I know where I've seen its sister . . . or should I say . . . its brother?'

'On a market stall? In a shop?' she teased him. She slipped the disc back under her shirt in case it caught on something and was lost.

'No, a black and silver sign of love, male and female, Yin and Yang . . . I saw it in the theatre.'

A hand touched her arm. 'Ready to go? I'll walk you back, Rosalind.' Peregrine smiled down at her. 'Better say goodnight to Anna, and get your coat.'

She murmured goodnight to the two other men and went to the kitchen. Alan King stared after her as if he had seen a ghost.

CHAPTER EIGHT

'I HATE sitting here packing swabs,' said Nurse Stephen gloomily.

'I'm inclined to agree,' Sister Rosalind Mason sighed. 'It seems such a waste of theatre time and if we can't have operations here, I'd rather be out in the sun. It's a lovely Easter so far and I envy people going away in the spring when the weather's good.'

She folded a towel that the junior had marked with red cotton with the name of the theatre, a time-consuming job that couldn't be left, as marking ink was either bleached out or made the marked area rotten and soon frayed.

'May I go for coffee?' asked Nurse Stephen.

'Both go and take your time. I'll have coffee here today and keep an eye on the theatre. I have to check the drug cupboard and I don't feel like breaking off in the middle. Go now and bring me my Sunday paper from my pigeon hole.' She thought for a minute. 'Is your boy friend still in London?'

'Yes, Sister. He goes back on Tuesday. He wanted me to go to the parade in Regent's Park, but I can't make it.'

'I think you should. You have some time owing to you and even if we get a case, it can be only something simple like a foreign body in the ear, or something that doesn't take much preparation. Mr

Murray is at home and can be contacted and I could go off for a while this evening, instead of this afternoon. Go now, ring your fiancé and he can pick you up in an hour.'

'Oh, thank you, Sister! I'll be back at tea time.'

'No hurry, I have no plans. Make it six-thirty and I shall be quite happy.' She watched the girl dance away and felt a pang of envy. She had seen Nurse Stephen's boy friend and he didn't arouse this feeling, but she was envious of the fact that the girl was loved by the man she loved.

The theatre seemed empty of everything but mocking sunlight and sterile cases of inhuman apparatus. The gallery was dark and bare and the trolleys were neatly aligned in rigid precision. Rosalind put coffee to simmer in the small steriliser and took a chair on to the balcony. It was half in sun and half in shade and the air was warm.

The coffee bubbled, adding a homely dimension to the odours of the theatre. The outer door swung open and Rosalind paused, coffee jug in hand. She blushed faintly. 'I smelled your coffee all the way from Casualty,' said Peregrine.

'I don't believe you, but it *is* fresh, I *do* have enough for two or three and I was just going to pour it.'

He sat on the wall overlooking the drive. 'Lovely day,' he said. She brought another of the supply of stacking chairs kept in a cupboard for visitors. 'Thanks, but I'll sit up here.'

'Well, be careful. I don't want to feature in a gruesome newspaper headline, "Theatre Sister Screams as Surgeon disappears over Parapet. Was he pushed or did he fall?"'

'Would you care?' He looked down at her as she poured the coffee and saw the golden glints in her hair.

'Of course I would. Nobody likes to be that notorious.' She handed him the cup and saucer with a steady hand. I'm getting quite good at being flippant with him, she thought.

'You're right . . . it wouldn't be fair to make a mess of your nice tidy life.'

'I don't think you would want to do that,' she said, gravely, handing him the biscuit tin.

'Are you always as cool, Rosalind? You are the perfect sister, efficient, good in an emergency and pleasant to your staff.'

'Thank you, sir.'

'And stop twitching the corners of your mouth. I know when you are really laughing at me, but only when you have no mask over your mouth.'

She tried to keep her lips under control, but the joy of having him near made her heart sing and her face relax into an absurd smile, or so it seemed to her. He felt in the pocket of his white coat and brought out a small comb.

'That's mine! Where did you find it?'

'Anna said she thought it belonged to you and asked me to return it. She told me not to forget and that you were on duty this morning, so here I am.'

'Thank you . . .' the sun seemed less bright. 'You were just passing?'

'No, I was coming here to collect a few things and to ask if Wendy was back.'

'Perry!' His name was out before she knew she had said it. 'I'm sure she'll be all right. I can understand how you feel about her bathing in that water, but surely, it would be a chance in a million for her to contract anything like meningitis or diphtheria?'

'I'm being a fool,' he said. 'What are you doing today? Not putting on your Easter bonnet to join the parade?'

'I never wear a bonnet . . . I've too much hair.'

'Not too much. I was glad when you lost your comb last night. It suits you better free.'

She hid her green eyes. 'I couldn't find it and forgot to ask Anna to look out for it. I have to keep my hair under control for duty and . . .'

'For tennis?' She glanced up, unsure of his tone, but he was smiling.

'Yes, for that, too, but I think I'll leave tennis balls in difficult places in future.'

'Not on my account, I enjoyed your visit. How are the scratches? Should be gone by now.' He made a movement towards her and she stepped back.

'They've healed perfectly, thank you. No further treatment needed.' If I didn't know differently, she thought, I'd say he was flirting with me. And yet he's thinking of the girl who died such a long while ago. Her heart ached for him. He was trying to be sociable while all the time he must compare every woman he met with the one love of his life who was now dead. She gave him more coffee, and noticed that he was wearing casual clothes.

As if in answer to her unspoken question, he said, 'I'm on my way to friends for lunch, but I shall be back this evening. I want to be near the hospital tonight so I shall sleep in the medical block.'

'But there are no cases due and Tony said he'd come if needed. You could go home.'

'Home? Oh, yes, so I could. I ought to go soon, but they can manage without me quite well.' He frowned. 'I shall be here, kicking my heels all the evening. Will you stop me dying of boredom and have dinner with me at the Falcon?'

'If you want me to.' She was taken by surprise. He more or less had to take her to Anna's party, but this was a free decision, even if it was made out of boredom. He left the theatre and she wondered who could do without him, who was at home, wherever home was, and if the people there were parents, a lover, or a dozen cats and dogs looked after by an old family retainer.

She was still daydreaming when the junior nurse came back to report on duty, closely followed by Alan King. Rosalind gave Nurse the job of turning out a cupboard by the door of the office and took a malicious delight in the look of disgust that Alan King gave to the trolley-load of packets of new rubber gloves that had to be counted before more were ordered. 'Does she have to do that now?' he said. 'I was hoping for a quiet chat alone with you.'

'Sorry. It's our only chance when there isn't a lot happening.' She looked up at him with innocent green eyes, but her lips twitched. 'We can chat quite well here and she isn't making enough noise to disturb us.'

'You really don't like me, do you, Ros?'

'I like you very much, Alan, but I have no intention of being another of your conquests.' She smiled. 'If you could forget that you are the answer to a maiden's prayer for five minutes, we could be very good friends . . . I'd even take up your invitation of a day on the river, but, knowing you, I don't think it would work.'

He walked round the office, lifting a book here, a paper there. He went on to the balcony and leaned over. 'At least we shan't be interrupted by Perry.' He waved, and shouted in an exaggerated American accent, 'Have a good day.' He swung down from the wall, chuckling. 'He saw me and boy! Did I get a black look!' He grinned and the light brown eyes were insolent. 'Perry doesn't like anyone muscling in on his territory.'

'He probably thinks you've come here to borrow something. Like phials of Thio-pentone, or lubricant.'

He laughed. 'At this moment, that's the least of his worries. Where has he gone?'

'How should I know?'

'I assume he came here to say goodbye before he went?'

'He came here, certainly, but only to return something I left at the party last night. Anna asked him to bring it to me.'

He looked at her sideways. 'Such an innocent smile the girl has . . . such guileless green eyes.'

'If you must talk in riddles, you'll have to excuse me. I have some work to do, even if you have all the time in the world.'

'Naughty temper. I was only saying what all the hospital will be saying soon, that you and Perry have something going between you.'

'What? You can't say that . . . it isn't true. Just because he took me to Anna's last night doesn't mean we even had a date. He was going there and offered to walk with me, that's all.' He was still grinning in an infuriating manner. 'If names were linked every time two people left here together, the hospital is just as likely to talk about you and me as anyone. After all, I was seen getting into your car . . . does that compromise me beyond redemption?'

'I wish it did, but like a perfect knight, I accept defeat gracefully. I must say that you two kept very quiet about it, but I think I know now whose sweater walked along the medical corridor, looking so . . . desirable.'

'You can't think that there is anything between us, it's ridiculous. You've seen just how rude he is sometimes in the theatre and how he treats me like a half-wit at times.' She stared at him, defiantly. 'Besides, he told me he was in love with someone . . . a girl who died a long time ago.'

'You mean the girl who contracted meningitis after swimming in an infected pool and inhaling the water?'

'You knew about it?'

He shrugged. 'I heard something, but it was before my time. I think a group of students went swimming . . . as they do, as you must have done . . . as I have done, but in their case it was in the remains of a hot well that bubbled into a gravel pit that formed a natural lake. One of them discovered it by chance when cycling in the countryside and they did it for a lark.'

'I don't understand, it was something that could have happened to anyone.'

'It was Perry who found the pool and he felt responsible.'

'And he still loves her,' said Rosalind, sadly.

'Ah, well, if that's true, and I don't say I believe it, there's hope for me yet. I'll take you on the river the first fine weekend that you are off-duty.'

She heard him try the locked cabinets in the anaesthetic room as he left. So he wasn't there just to see her! She smiled, grimly. Alan would take what he could from the theatre to use on his own private patients, he would take any pleasure he could find, where he found it, and he would take and use her if she let him do so. She tried to concentrate on her books, but the face of Peregrine Bradford rose before her. He looked sad and she knew that while she might have stood a chance of gaining his attention with a living rival, there was no rivalry with the dead that she could fight and win.

'If you've finished, you can go to lunch,' she told the nurse. That's all I seem to do today, send nurses off duty, see them back on duty and sit here pretending to do my books, she thought. The Sunday paper was full of the usual nitty-gritty of politics and scandal, the fashion pages told her that she would be wearing what looked to her like the most unwearable clothes she'd seen for years and that hair would be worn short and frizzy. 'Big deal,' she said. 'I'm having my hair cut for no-one.' The day wore on and she was glad to see her staff nurse's smiling face appear at six o'clock. 'Have a good day?' she said, and recalled Alan King shouting the same phrase to Peregrine Bradford, with a slightly different intonation.

'Wonderful . . . it's the first time I've seen the horses parading in Regent's Park. Lots of people were dressed up and I saw my first Pearly King and Queen. I didn't know they dressed like that any more, but someone said that they handed the costumes down from parents to children and the original pearl buttons made of genuine mother-of-pearl make them valuable.' Rosalind listened indulgently, thinking how little it took to amuse a girl in love.

'Nothing happening here, so it's just as well you took the time off. I'll go now.'

'Are you going out, Sister?'

'Yes . . . I suppose I am,' she said, slowly. As she walked across to the home, she wondered why she had said she'd go to dinner with Peregrine—he can't really want me there, unless he is very sick of his own company. She went listlessly to her room to bath and change and dressed in a soft jersey suit of pale green. It wasn't new but it was comfortable and she had forgotten that it made her eyes echo the gentle colour. She slipped on the jacket over a shirt of orchid pink and brushed out her hair, leaving it free after the restricting cap and ties worn all day. She heard the telephone ring downstairs and hurried down, in case it was Perry ringing.

'Hello . . . That *is* Rosalind?'

'Wendy? Where are you? Are you all right?'

'Of course, why shouldn't I be all right? There's

been no rail disaster, no motorway crash, no hijack that I know of here.'

'Oh, nothing . . . I just thought you were back soon.'

'I'm not back yet, I rang to say that I was expecting a parcel. Could you nip up to my room and see if it's there.'

Rosalind ran up and saw a parcel on the bed. 'It's there,' she said.

'Good. I can tell the person who sent it that it's safe. I needn't write to confirm it when I get back.'

'When do you arrive?'

'I've decided to come back tonight and meet my friends again in London, tomorrow. The Roman thing wasn't all that exciting . . . all a bit mucky, I thought.'

'But you did swim?' Rosalind hoped that her anxiety couldn't be heard.

'Oh yes, I dived in and it wasn't bad, but some of them chickened out and didn't bother. See you . . . I've no more change.' The pips sounded and Rosalind went slowly back to her room. It was silly to feel anxious, but she couldn't forget the expression on Peregrine's face when he heard of Wendy's Roman weekend. She sounded cheerful enough and Wendy is very tough, of course she's all right, she told herself for the tenth time.

It was less than half an hour before she heard the front door bell and went down to find Peregrine waiting. As usual, her heart lurched when she saw him standing there, elegant in a silk roll-neck sweater of pale grey under a velvet jacket of jet black. The tight, well tailored trousers gave an air of expensive simplicity and he was smiling. Rosalind decided to forget about Wendy and the fact that she would be back at the hospital that night. If anything should happen, I shall know she's in the best place possible, but there's no need to spoil the evening by getting worked up over events beyond my control.

'Hello,' she said, 'you're very punctual.'

'Shall we walk through the park? It's a lovely evening. Everywhere I went today there were people out enjoying themselves . . . It's nice to see families taking picnics in the country.' They talked of the part of Surrey where he had friends, but he didn't mention his own home. 'The beech woods are wonderful just now . . . you should come down sometime,' he said, casually.

'I like Surrey,' she said. The park was clearing as children were taken home, tired and sometimes cross after a day in the sun. The magnolias were blooming, with great waxen flowers on the bare branches scenting the air. Rosalind picked up a flower dropped by a child who had torn it from a branch. She smoothed the petals and inhaled the delicate fragrance, her cheeks matching the pink and white pallor of the bloom. Across the sky the white line of frozen exhaust followed a plane high above them and the trees sighed. I should be happy here, wandering in this pretty place with the man who I have come to want more than anyone on earth, she thought, but the evening sadness seeped into her soul and when she glanced at the stern profile above her, she knew that the one thing they shared was sadness.

The restaurant was fairly crowded but they were shown to a table that he had booked earlier. To her surprise, Rosalind found that she was enjoying his almost silent company and there was no need for animated conversation. From time to time, they talked of people they both knew and he gradually became more talkative. 'What was Alan doing this morning?'

'He wanted to borrow, I think, but I had locked all the cupboards as the theatre wasn't being used.' She smiled. 'I think I'm a great disappointment to him. He has to buy everything he needs for use outside, now.'

'I hope you disappoint him in other ways, too.' His smile was wry.

'I think I do. He's very good company and if he'd realise that women do *not* expect a man to make a pass every time they meet, we'd get on fine.'

'When you are in uniform, it would take a very brave or foolish man to make any such pass at you, Sister Rosalind. You are the epitome of the perfect dedicated career-woman with no time for dalliance.' His eyes were deeply blue, his voice low. She fluttered eyelids that hoped to hide the tenderness in her own eyes. 'And, with your hair like that . . . any man with red blood in his veins must want you.'

She looked up, amazed. He was looking at her with a mixture of sadness and longing. 'I shall have to look for a man with red blood,' she said.

'You should have no trouble,' he said. 'You get on well with men of your own age . . . I've noticed.'

'I get bored with students,' she said, softly, but

he had turned to the waiter who was asking if he knew if Mr Bradford was in the room.

'Excuse me,' said Perry, putting down his table napkin. 'Don't go away.' He smiled and she sat lost in the warmth and tenderness he left behind him. Her eyes grew moist. If only . . . another moment and he might have . . . what? Propositioned her? He hadn't mentioned love. She shook herself free of such thoughts. He was just making the sort of remarks that, as he would have said, any red-blooded man would make.

He came back, looking annoyed. 'Anything wrong?' she asked.

'There's been a fight in one of the parks. They've taken four youths into Cas. and one has a broken nose.'

'You don't deal with cases like that do you?'

'Not as a rule, but this one has a piece of glass in his right maxillary antrum. The HS is scared of doing more harm than good and I agree with him. I can do it in Cas. Major, but I'll need some things from Theatre.'

'I'll come too. It will be quicker. You can tell me what you think you'll need as we go.' At once, they were completely professional, the lighter moments lost, perhaps for ever.

'Great. I asked them to send a taxi. We ought to get there fast as he's bleeding and they can't plug before we get the foreign body removed.'

The taxi whisked them back to Beattie's and they parted at the entrance to Casualty. Rosalind fled up the stairs to the theatre, her keys ready in her hand, almost grabbed from the rack in the night porter's office. Quickly, she put a drum of sterile instruments and sutures on a trolley and added several likely items that seemed necessary. She rushed it all to the lift and was in Casualty within minutes of going to the theatre. 'Come on . . . hurry,' said Mr Bradford, 'We haven't got all day.' He saw that Rosalind was putting on a mask. 'Good, we can do with all the help we can get. The other cubicles are full and we'll have to manage this one. Give Sister a gown.'

He proceeded to examine the youth who lay in panic-stricken shock at the sight of his own blood and not the blood of the ones he was fighting. 'Broken bottles?' said Rosalind.

'Stupid young fools. They watch too many gang films and when they're hurt, they can't believe it.' His hands worked gently, all the time he grumbled under his breath and Rosalind swabbed and handed instruments until the jagged sliver of glass came away, followed by a gush of fresh blood. 'We'd better seal some of these bleeding points before we set the septum.' Soon, the nose was more or less in the shape it had been born, but swollen and very discoloured. The nasal plugging was in place making it necessary for all breathing to be done by mouth, but the bleeding had stopped and as Rosalind cleaned up the boy's face and the brightly-dyed hair that was matted with blood and mud, she saw that he was very young, very sorry for himself and bore no resemblance to the youth who had taken his courage from being with a gang of his own age and kind.

'He'll have to be admitted,' said Peregrine. He

looked down at the soaking front of his gown, awash with saline and blood. 'Damn,' he said. 'I wanted to go up to the ward with him.'

'Change the gown,' said Rosalind, giving him a fresh one. She helped him with the tapes of the soiled one and took it from him. His silk shirt was badly soiled, but he covered it with the clean gown and went with the boy. Rosalind helped the casualty staff to clear the cubicle and gathered up the items from her own department. She saw Peregrine come back to take his jacket from the office. 'You can't put that on over the shirt . . . it's very bloody.' She hesitated. 'I could fetch another from your room.'

'Good idea, I can't very well walk about with no shirt. He handed her a key. 'Top drawer, right, any Tee-shirt will do. And, Rosalind . . . we still have time to have that coffee we missed.'

She smiled, understanding the change of mood form the man intent on an important and urgent case who swore and was impatient, to this wonderful man who smiled at her, making her eyes light up with pleasure.

She brought the shirt and ran back with it. He glanced at her heightened colour and the fast breathing. 'You needn't kill yourself . . . but I'm grateful.' He peeled off the soiled silk shirt and rubbed his chest with it to dry the skin underneath.

Rosalind held the clean garment in nerveless hands. She stared at the talisman that lay on the fine dark hairs of his broad chest . . . the talisman that lay face downwards with the motif now hidden. But it had spun round as he held out his arms to put them into the sleeves of the fresh shirt and there was a flash of silver and black, in roughly equal parts. It was impossible to say that it was a Yin Yang emblem, but it was impossible to say that it wasn't.

'Mr Bradford . . .' said a nurse. 'Sister Fletcher rang and asked for you. She said you left a message for her to contact you.'

He went swiftly to the internal telephone and Rosalind followed him. 'Perry here,' he said. 'I wondered if you'd like to come for a drink with Rosalind and me.' His voice was controlled and easy. 'Why not?' he added, sharply.

He listened and Rosalind saw his face change. He spoke a few words and slammed down the receiver. 'What is it?' she said, her face pale with apprehension.

'It may be nothing . . . I pray to God it's nothing.'

'What did she say?' She ran to catch up with him.

'Nurse, take these back to the theatre for me and put them in my office,' she said, crisply and ran after the man who was already striding away to the Nurses' Home with a look of thunder on his brow.

He paused by the lift and waited for her. 'She said she wouldn't come because she had a headache.' He looked into her eyes and took a deep breath 'I'm glad you're here, Ros . . . we must play it cool and not let her know we suspect that she might be ill.' He took her cold hands in his as the lift stopped. 'You've no idea how glad I am to have you with me.' He kissed her, gently, and put a hand to touch the honey-gold locks that fell freely. 'Come on, act as if we've just come to say hello.'

CHAPTER NINE

'I CAN'T believe it.' Rosalind Mason put down the telephone and turned to her staff nurse. 'Sister Fletcher is out of danger and taking notice.' She smiled a little shakily. 'It's only seven days since she was diagnosed and the treatment was begun and now it's nearly over.'

'That's what comes of prompt action, Sister. If you and Mr Bradford hadn't been two jumps ahead, she might have died, and that would have been tragic.'

Rosalind looked round the theatre and was glad that she had been busy with Tony Murray's lists during the past day or so. She told the theatre staff to get the instruments washed and put away and suddenly she was tired. She thought back to the night when Sister Wendy Fletcher had telephoned and said she had a headache. Rosalind could almost hear the voice of Peregrine Bradford again as he asked Wendy, so gently, if her head was very bad.

'Not like the headaches I have with a period, Perry. I can't understand it. I'm not really the headachy sort.'

He had glanced at Rosalind. 'How long have you had it?' she asked. 'Have you something Wendy can take, Perry?' She made it sound as if she was asking for Aspirin or some simple remedy and he nodded. Rosalind went to the girl sitting on the edge of her bed looking pale and vaguely unwell. She touched her as if by accident and Wendy drew away, sharply. Perry looked grave. 'You don't look very well,' said Rosalind. 'Any pain?' They had both noticed her heightened reaction to touch.

'I feel a bit as if I have 'flu coming. I might have caught a cold dressed in that stupid white dress I wore. It was warm in the bath place, but the dining room was not all that warm.' She shivered, but when Rosalind took her hand it was hot. 'I'm a bit stiff . . . must have been a draught somewhere.' Perry came closer and looked into her eyes. Even during the short time they were in the room, she had changed.

'Ring Charles Bing and get him here at once,' whispered Peregrine. Rosalind fled and minutes later, the physician was holding Wendy's wrist and looking grave. 'Well?' said Peregrine.'

'Knowing the history, I think you're right. Wendy?' She turned dull eyes towards him. 'I want you warded. You've caught a bug.' She nodded as if she couldn't care what they did to her and when the stretcher arrived, she lay still, and asked no questions. The rest followed, the lumbar puncture and quick diagnosis from the smear of cerebo-spinal fluid taken and rushed to the pathological department, and the swift start to treatment with antibiotics suitable for meningitis. By morning, the arrested condition was stable, in a few more hours it was slightly better and responding all the time.

Rosalind had kept away, had bathed and been given a throat spray after which a throat swab was taken the following day so that she could be pronounced free of infection and able to work again in the theatre. Peregrine Bradford had done the same and they followed Wendy's progress eagerly.

'They've cordoned off the spa and the hotel and no one is allowed there until the place has a clean bill of health. Wendy was the only one who dived and took in some of the water through her nose. The organisms went quickly through the soft tissues and got into the lining of the brain.'

'What would have happened if she had gone to bed and and stayed there the next day? It was her time off and no one would have checked unless she didn't keep an appointment?' said Nurse Stephen.

'It doesn't bear thinking about. If Mr Bradford hadn't had a sixth sense about it because . . . he had met a similar case, she might have died.' She tried to smile. 'But it's fairly easy to cure now. When did you last hear of anyone dying of meningitis?'

'I've never met a case at all until now, Sister.'

'So it doesn't do to get too scared of the condition. It can be treated and if taken early leaves no after-affects. I'm longing to see her, but they'll have to make sure she isn't going to be a carrier first.'

Tony Murray emerged from the surgeon's room. 'Seen Perry?' He ran a hand through his hair and straightened his tie. 'No? He said he would bring in some things I wanted. He may leave them at the lodge. If he comes here with them, would you get them downstairs so that I can collect them tomorrow without coming up here?'

'I wasn't expecting him,' said Rosalind. He had collected all his special instruments and microscope to use in the nursing home when his overseas visitors came to watch his operating technique. That had been two days ago and she had seen him only once since Wendy was taken to the isolation ward.

She lingered in the dining room and let the general conversation wash over her. He had no reason to visit the theatre. He had no case there for another two days and he could check Wendy's condition with Charles Bing in whose charge she was still being treated. The tiny shafts of light that had brightened her meetings with him were extinguished and she knew that if he could now forget about Wendy, he would slip back into this worship of the girl who died from the same disease. If he married, it would be someone to help him in his profession and not for reasons of passion. Even during the moments when he showed that he was attracted to her, she knew that he found her too young and superficial for him to take seriously. Good for a small dinner party, even if they didn't finish it, good for a party given by mutual friends, if pushed into it, but she was not good enough to be with him . . . in his arms and heart as lover and wife.

She looked in the outer rooms, mechanically checking that everything was in place and the theatre was ready for action. Whatever she might think or suffer, the routine must be meticulously followed to make sure that no mistake was ever made, no unavoidable risk taken in the well-ordered and efficient department. As soon as one case was over, the theatre had no breathing space for its staff until every instrument was clean, every pack restored and the trolleys were ready to be laid with whatever equipment would be required at little notice. It had become such a ritual that sometimes Rosalind thought she could tell what was wrong or what hadn't been done just by standing in the doorway and sniffing the air-conditioned atmosphere!

Nobody had talked much during the past few days. Wendy's illness had shaken the staff badly, and the sense of relief at her recovery was only now showing through the anxiety. Even Alan King had stopped being facetious and seemed genuinely concerned. Rosalind found his gaze disconcerting as she went about her duties and he was at the head of the operating table administering gases. He had changed and his gaze was no longer full of snide appraisal, but more filled with affection and resignation. There was sadness, too, and she had a feeling that sadness was a feature in the members of staff in the ENT theatre. Even Nurse Stephens went about with a miserable face now that her fiancé had gone back to Germany where he was stationed in a helicopter unit.

Rosalind went into her office, but could find no excuse for staying longer on duty. The evening lay ahead, empty of everything but her own thoughts. Footsteps came along the corridor and Alan King came in. 'Heard the news? Wendy is clear.'

'I know . . . it's terrific. She'll have time off and should be back on duty quite soon. Now that she is getting bored, I must collect up some magazines for her.'

He sat on the corner of the desk on the spot where she had left her medallion—was it such a little while ago? Instinctively, her hand went to the disc that she could feel through the thin material of her uniform dress. He noticed the gesture. 'You haven't seen much of him since Wendy crocked up, have you?'

'Who?'

'Lover boy . . . come off it, Ros. You may be as much of a dark horse as he is, but I saw it, remember.'

'I don't know what you're talking about, Alan. Saw what?'

'You showed me your Yin Yang thing.'

'And you said you'd seen one like it in the theatre. Now, I suppose you'll produce it with an air of innocence as if you hadn't taken it from that very desk!' Her sarcasm was mixed with mild irritation. It was all so trivial, this bantering flirtatious manner that he thought women liked.

He stared and then burst out laughing. 'You must keep a supply of them. I like that . . . Oh, yes, I think that's very rich.' He laughed even more at her complete bewilderment. 'You are either very dumb or you are a first-class actress, Ros. But seriously, when did you exchange love tokens? Don't pretend that you don't know what Perry wears round his neck these days?'

She grew pale. How could Alan make fun of what must be a sacred memory? 'He wears a medallion, a talisman in memory of the girl who died of meningitis. The one that you took might look similar—I've no idea as I haven't seen his medallion clearly—but I didn't give it to him, if that's what you are insinuating.'

'You really don't know?' His wonderment was complete. 'Well, well, you should take a look sometime.' He sighed. 'But why I should tell you, I have no idea.' He smiled, sadly, 'Except that I know that you and I will never make it, Ros.' He put up a hand as she seemed about to speak. 'You're the first woman I really wanted, after my separation. Yes, don't look so surprised. Surely it was rumoured? I married five years ago and she didn't like it here. I think she missed her family in Australia.'

'And you don't love her?'

'That is in the melting pot . . . we parted and I was very angry. I thought I could have a good life without her, but now that I know I can't have you, selfish it may be, but I'm grabbing what I can of marriage and . . . comfort.' He examined his finger nails. 'I was shattered when I saw Wendy and it suddenly made me want to go to Australia and patch it up.'

'And when do you go? Or is this another little-boy-lost ploy for sympathy?'

'This is for real. I even rang Australia House to see what my prospects there would be and they welcomed me with open arms. I can hardly believe it. I have a job waiting as soon as I can make arrangements.'

'And . . . your wife?'

He seemed faintly embarrassed. 'She seems to welcome the idea too. She is giving me one more chance if I settle down and become a family man.'

Rosalind giggled. 'I can see you wandering in the outback with six or seven children.'

'Don't. It makes me weak to think of it, but I think I need it.' He put his hands on her shoulders and bent to kiss her.' He sighed.'I thought that kiss would be "hello", but it's really "goodbye."'

'Goodbye, Alan, I shall see you here when we're working, but we may never have time again. Be happy . . . and send me a Christmas card.'

'I'll never do that,' he said. She reached up and gently kissed his cheek. 'Thank you for that,' he said and left quickly.

So even Alan was coming to grips with life. We all have our places, she thought, and tried to tell herself that her lot was all that she could desire, but the wall of sadness that had formed between her and Perry was high and inpenetrable. He will waste his life cherishing a dream and I shall become a very good chief nursing officer; but the prospect held little comfort for her.

The dining room was full of the news of Sister Fletcher's wonderful recovery and Anna Forsythe was already planning a welcome-back party for her as soon as she was fit. 'By the way, Rosalind, I was talking to Perry and asked him to meet us after dinner at the Falcon. I'm going home first and Slade is eating at St Thomas's, but he should be back soon.' She glanced at Rosalind's pale face. 'You look as if you need a change. I thought you did at lunch, so I asked Perry to bring you this evening if you've nothing better to do.'

'I . . . don't know. I haven't thought about this

evening. I haven't seen Perry. Perhaps he has other plans.'

Anna looked at her more closely. 'We are all concerned about Wendy, but in a way I think it's laid a few ghosts. It proves how well these infections can be treated and it has alerted the authorities to the dangers of letting private concerns promote such places without due care.' She smiled. 'Come if you can, but don't feel you have to. I like people to drop in if they feel like it, but I know that sometimes it's good to be alone.'

Rosalind went up to the isolation ward and saw Wendy through a glass screen. It was not really necessary to be so cautious now, but anyone working in a theatre where infection could do damage to patients needed to be extra careful. Wendy looked bright and bored and welcomed the magazines, threatening to run away if they didn't allow her out soon. 'You must be better,' said a deep voice into the intercom: Rosalind looked round and saw Peregrine Bradford standing behind her.

'How long have you been there?'

'Long enough to see that you've chatted and said all you have to say and we should leave her to sleep.'

Rosalind smiled and shrugged as if she had no control over him. His breath was on her hair and she was glad that she wore uniform and a businesslike hair style. He admitted that I look unapproachable dressed like this, she thought, and the knowledge gave her poise. I mustn't ever let him see my true feelings if we are to work together in the future. She gathered her cloak about her.

'Are you joining us, tonight?' The invitation was polite and light.

'I was going to wash my hair . . . there's nothing really specific planned, is there?'

'Ouch! Now I know that you hate me.' The jest was half-hearted, as if he thought it might be true.

'Anna mentioned meeting in the Falcon, but everyone was so busy talking about Wendy that I took it as a polite "if you're passing" kind of arrangement.'

'It is, and we shall. Get changed and I'll be downstairs in half an hour.'

'Are you asking me or telling me?' She tried to make her lip jut aggressively, but the edges were too sweet.

'Telling you. I think it's time someone told you what to do. I get tired of dominant females who know their own minds. I'm starting a campaign to bring the poor old male chauvinist back into being.'

'I wasn't aware that he'd ever gone out of fashion,' she said, scathingly. 'I'll take a tape recording of you one day when you're in your anti-everything mood in the theatre.'

He laughed. 'That's better. I began to think you were weakening. Don't do that until I see you again.'

She stared after him, wondering why his step was light and he looked so happy. The sight of his broad shoulders silhouetted against the evening light made her aware of his strength. I'm a fool to go with him, she thought. I shall only make myself miserable being there with him and knowing that I can never be loved by him. She wondered if Alan

wasn't wiser than she to accept what he could get
and cut his losses. She cast her mind back to
students who had wanted her. She recalled the
pleasure of flirting with men who wanted only a
good time but had no designs on her for keeps. She
could no longer bring into focus the face of the
patient she had once loved and knew that he was a
wraith from the past who had no power to trouble
her or even to invade her dreams.

Other images did that, and they were all of the
same man. Other shapes were as shadows, but he
was real and all powerful. She brushed her hair and
picked up the constricting side combs, but put them
down again. If I wear them, I shall give the signal
that I am unapproachable . . . the type of stand-
offish female he was hinting at, and if I wear my hair
loose, at least I can shake it forward and hide in
moments of shyness or use it to hide my eyes. She
put on the pale grey velvet which would go any-
where, from a private party to a night club, and still
be suitable for lounging about in the Falcon.

She went downstairs to wait and to her surprise
he was already there. He eyed her clothes with
approval and she saw that he was wearing the velvet
jacket again with a pale blue silk roll neck similar to
the one that he had to take off when it was stained
with blood and water in the cubicle in Casualty
Major. 'What happened to the boy with the glass in
his antrum?' she said, to keep talking.

'Oh, he spent a very uncomfortable week in the
ward. Talking and breathing through the mouth at
the same time makes life difficult, especially if you
are a truculent youth who is more used to sounding

off at others than to listening.' Perry grinned. 'It might have done him good. He had to listen and let others tell him what they thought and he also learned that we didn't care a damn for his image but were anxious to make him well again. Perhaps he will take a little of it with him when he next joins a gang.'

'Has he gone home?'

'Yes. He comes in for washouts and drops, but he will have a pretty good nose when it's all settled.'

'Where are we going? It's a fine evening. We can walk to Anna's as we did the last time.'

'You aren't on call, are you?' She shook her head. 'Neither am I, and this time I have no intention of sitting on the end of a telephone line. We'll give Anna a miss tonight.'

'But she'll be expecting us.'

'I think not.' He opened the door of a low-slung sports care and indicated the passenger seat. 'Let's get the smell of this place out of our nostrils and find a quiet spot.' She sat in the car obediently and could think of nothing to say and no excuse that would let her stay away from him or be with a crowd of friends in which she could lose her personality.

'It's nice to know where I'm going,' she said.

'Don't be so inquisitive. You'll know when we get there.'

'You sound like my aunt. She can't get used to the fact that I'm a grown woman.'

'Are you, Rosalind? Are you a grown woman?' He looked stern in the flickering lights of the roadway. They eased out of London into less busy roads and she knew they were heading in the general direction of the Thames, but further away than the stretch that she knew.

'Of course I am. I am fully qualified for my work, I think I run the theatre efficiently, and I am all set for an interesting career.' She hoped that the dimness inside the car hid the trembling of her mouth.

'You do all of that, but when I am with you like this, I feel that you are so young. . . so very young.'

She sank back with her hair about her face. He was trying to tell her he found her efficient, good to work with and good company . . . but too immature to consider as anything more. Well, she would have to accept it. In a way it was easier to know where she stood in his estimation. She took a deep breath and tried to laugh. 'You make me feel about ten when you talk like that. There are some men who make me feel older. Some even treat me like a grown woman.'

'Men like King?'

'Yes, even Alan. Believe it or not, it's quite pleasant to be told I look good and to know that he thinks I'm attractive.' She grew reckless. 'I'm very fond of Alan. He might be a bit of a heel sometimes, but he has heart.'

She glanced at his profile and wondered if he would take her words as a personal insult, but she couldn't read his expression.

'Well, it looks as if you are going to lose your admirer.'

'I know,' she said, and relapsed into silence.

'Don't you mind?' he asked, cautiously.

'It's always sad to lose good friends, but some of

us don't make it a lifetime's obsession,' she said, bitterly.

'We're there,' he said, quietly.

He stopped the car in the driveway of a small house overlooking the river. The pale tower of Windsor etched its outline against the sky and a late bird scolded on its way home. A dim light from the hall was the only sign of life and she followed him as he walked briskly to the front door. 'Do I know the people?' she whispered.

'Not well enough,' he whispered back and took keys from his pocket. She watched, wide-eyed, as he unlocked the front door and the hall was flooded with soft light. He picked up a few letters from the floor and put them on the table with another pile of mail. 'I come to collect mail,' he said, 'but we can make coffee if you like or go on to the pub down the road.'

'You live here?' She looked about her at the velvet curtains, the thick luxurious carpet and the glowing silver in a graceful cabinet. She followed him into a long room that had a window the whole length of the wall overlooking the river. Long glass doors opened on to a wide lawn that swept down to the water and in the sky hung an infant moon. This room was furnished sparcely but with good taste. It was modern with clean lines and clear colours, as if she had stepped from an old-fashioned house in the hall to another dimension of all that was best in current fashion. 'It's lovely,' she said.

'I keep it on and even thought I might have the whole place tidied up. This is the first room I had done.'

She saw the newness of the hangings, the freshness of the rugs and thought that it had been a very recent innovation. 'It belonged to a relative . . . I have no living family . . . except for one cousin. A housekeeper looks after this place and cares for my friends when they stay here. Her son looks after the collection of birds that was left with the house. Come and see.'

She followed him into a glass-walled annexe and saw that on every side were wide cages of budgerigars and canaries. He looked at them without enthusiasm.

'You don't really like them, do you?' she said.

'I hate to see birds in cages,' he said. 'You don't like to see them either!'

'It's always been my wish to free every bird in a cage but I can see that it's not so bad if they are bred in captivity. Are you going to keep them?'

'They have been here for a long time and I know the lad who looks after them loves them. In fact . . . I've told him to look on them as his own. It brings someone to the house to keep an eye on it when the housekeeper isn't here and he could never afford an aviary like this.'

'Perhaps you should give them to Alan to take with him.'

'Alan? What do you mean? I heard he was leaving quite suddenly, but he was very unwilling to talk about it.'

'He's joining his wife in Australia.' She watched the glow fade from his eyes. 'He's found a job there and is going to be a good pillar of society and raise a family.'

'But I thought he was leaving for . . . other personal reasons. I had no idea he was still in love with his wife.'

'I think he is,' said Rosalind, but her heart was almost choking her as she saw his unease.

'And you, do you mind that he's going?'

'No, of course not. I never tangle with married men and I knew he didn't really care for me.'

'You know that's not true. I was convinced that he was leaving because he loved you very much.'

She lowered her eyelids. 'He's made a very wise decision,' she said, firmly.

'Coffee,' he said, breaking a taut silence which threatened to suffocate them. 'In here. I make very good coffee.'

'So I don't have to put on an apron and do the domestic bit,' she said, lightly.

'If I thought I'd get away with it, I'd try, but you are a very emancipated girl, Rosalind.'

'Let's compromise. Where do you keep cups or mugs or silver beakers . . . flower pots, anything to drink out of?'

He pointed to a cupboard and she laid a tray with fine china and silver jugs, while he poured hot water through the coffee filter. They sat in the long room facing the dim water, the curtains widely open and only a rose-shaded lamp in the corner. He put on a disc and Rosalind felt a lump in her throat as the Chopin Nocturne that had haunted her dreams since the night she had been at the concert and heard it when he was there, came softly and sadly through the warm silence. She accepted a liqueur with the coffee and tried to enjoy the moment, acutely aware of the man who sat by her on the long pastel-tweed covered settle.

She poured more coffee and handed it to him. His hand brushed her own and she trembled, spilling a little coffee in the saucer. 'I'm sorry, you see, I'm not used to fine bone china. After the thick cups in the dining room, these are very delicate.' She smiled tremulously, hoping that she wasn't about to make a complete fool of herself. 'I can't think why Alan didn't tell you where he was going. Surely it will be all over the hospital tomorrow?'

'I think he might have told me, but he was too intent on clearing up a misunderstanding.'

'Oh . . . he wanted to leave his own record clean in the theatre? What was it this time? Did he take more equipment and conveniently forget to bring it back?'

'No, it was something more personal.' He took her cup and put it back on the tray and moved closer. 'He seemed to think that he had misjudged a situation between you and me.'

She looked up, her eyes like a flash of green feathers from the startled birds next door. 'What do you mean? We've agreed to work together well and I'm happy about it.'

'He said that you wear a disc . . . a talisman.'

'Yes,' she sounded breathless. 'I bought it in the market to replace one I thought that Alan had taken. I intended making him think that it wasn't mine that he'd taken.'

'He thought that we had exchanged tokens . . . hidden tokens of love.'

'How ridiculous. He saw my disc and must have

known that it wasn't the same as yours, if, as you say, he saw the one you wear; and I know that you wear that because it is all that is left of the girl you loved . . . who died.' His eyes were unfathomable and in them she thought was deep pain. She put a soft hand on his arm. 'Can't you look on Wendy's recovery—due entirely to you and your precognition of evil, stemming from your earlier tragedy—as something that was cathartic, purging you of any former guilt for something over which you had no control. Can't you forget?'

'I was once conscious that I might have been partly responsible for the accident, but I never felt as deeply as you seem to think I did. I was in love, as puppies love, and I mourned for a friend, then work took over and I have not had the time to fall in love again.' He touched the sensuous velvet sleeve. She shivered slightly. 'I was looking for a dream . . . for perfection. Most of the women I meet are experienced and hard, or not as I want them in some way. The nurses get younger every year and most of the sisters are married or engaged, or living in . . . I think the expression is now.'

'But you meet lots of beautiful girls.'

'I was hoping for the impossible, a girl who was also a woman, with lovely hair and a beautiful face, a sweet nature and innocent eyes in which I could see the reflection of my soul. Show me your medallion, Rosalind.'

As if in a hypnotic state, she withdrew the slender chain from under her shirt and held the disc on the palm of her hand. He undid the chain from his own neck and held the twin to her Yin Yang symbol to match it. 'But how did you get one like it . . . it looks exactly the same as mine?'

'You left it on your desk and it fell into my shoes that I had to change in your office because a very up-tight and bossy little theatre sister made me do so before I went into the corridor. I found something very uncomfortable when I came to change again and this is what I found.'

'But you didn't say you had it. You must have known I'd miss it.'

'I put it in my pocket, not really knowing what it represented, until later.' The deep blue eyes gazed into the green misted ones. 'I saw that it was the sign of love, my talisman to touch when things go wrong, to bring me comfort when I'm alone, and as I said, the only thing I had belonging to the girl I love.'

'But I thought . . .'

His mouth found hers and stopped the trembling of her lips. A cloud of honey-gold hair fell over them and through it she knew there were stars that would light their way through life . . . and love and deepest desire.

For a moment, she struggled for the last vestiges of sanity, telling herself that this wasn't true, it couldn't happen to her, but she was powerless to do anything but sink closer in his arms, to feel the deep true beat of his heart and to know that he loved her with all the fervour and enduring passion of a man who had waited . . . for the perfect love . . . the love of his life, and she was all that he desired.

Her hands caressed the back of his head, finding

the stormy hair soft and warm, her body tensed to be at one with his—the Yin Yang of existence, the union of heart that no other person could sever.